CW00860081

LOVE'S MEMORY

LOVE'S MAGIC SERIES BOOK 12

BETTY MCLAIN

Copyright (C) 2020 Betty McLain

Layout design and Copyright (C) 2020 by Next Chapter

Published 2020 by Liaison – A Next Chapter Imprint

Edited by Elizabeth N. Love

Cover art by Cover Mint

This book is a work of fiction. Names, characters, places, and incidents are the product of the author's imagination or are used fictitiously. Any resemblance to actual events, locales, or persons, living or dead, is purely coincidental.

All rights reserved. No part of this book may be reproduced or transmitted in any form or by any means, electronic or mechanical, including photocopying, recording, or by any information storage and retrieval system, without the author's permission.

This book is dedicated to Love's Memory,
And to all who never forgot to remember first love.

CHAPTER 1

*I*t had been ten years since Silas Long Feather had last seen the young white girl spying on him and Jamie when they had stopped at a pond to swim. He had been nineteen, and Jamie was twenty-one.

The first time he saw her, they had been to Rolling Fork to make a delivery for the lumber yard. It was a very hot day, and when he spotted the pond through the trees, he had talked Jamie into stopping to cool off with a swim. They had swimming trunks in the truck with them after forgetting to take them out when they had gone swimming last.

They had changed and were running toward the water when Silas had felt eyes staring at him. He stopped and glanced around, spotting her in the trees. When he looked her way, she quickly hid behind the trees. Silas grinned and ran on and jumped into the water. The girl stayed there in the trees and watched until they started out of the water. She slipped away when they started toward their truck.

Silas smiled to himself. She had been cute, but he knew he could get into trouble if he was messing around with a young white girl. He did not tell Jamie about seeing the girl.

He didn't know why. He usually shared everything with Jamie, but for some reason, he was reluctant to share this with Jamie.

The rest of the summer, every time they made a trip to Rolling Fork, they would stop and go for a swim on the way home. Sometimes Silas would spot the girl watching them, and sometimes she would not be there. He began to look forward to seeing her hiding in the trees watching him. He did not know why he was so sure she was watching him and not Jamie, but he was sure. He had felt her eyes following his every move. He could feel her eyes caressing his body. She never approached them. She always stayed hidden and she would slip away when they left the water.

The weather started to cool off, too cool for swimming. Silas missed stopping and he missed seeing the girl in the trees. He looked carefully when they passed the spot, but he never saw her in the trees. He didn't know who she was, and he could not make inquiries about her because he was Indian and she was white.

The next summer, they began stopping for a swim again, but there was never any sign of the girl. Silas pushed the memory of her to the back of his mind and kept it there safe and sound from the world's intrusion.

May Flower Merril finished recording the deposition on her desk computer and carried the paper file to the filing cabinet to put it in its proper place. She was so ready for her lunch break. Now, if she could just slip out before Carlson knew she was leaving. Carlson followed her around and continued to try and convince her to marry him. She told him "no." She refused to date him, but it did not stop him from going to her family and getting them on his side. None of them paid any attention to her when she told them she was not in love with Carlson. All they saw was a big shot lawyer wanted to marry into the family, and they pushed his case constantly. The only one to seem less in favor of Carlson was her brother, Gunner.

May had moved out into her apartment to get away from all of the pressure. Her family thought she was making a big mistake. They were just as upset as they were when she dropped Flower out of her name and just used May. They couldn't understand all of the teasing she had endured being called May Flower. For a girl as shy as May had been, it had been agonizing.

When May slipped out of the office, somehow managing to avoid Carlson, she ran into her friend Brenda Oaks outside on the street.

"Hi, May, you're late for lunch break. It's already two-thirty," said Brenda.

"I know. I had a deposition I had to record. I'm taking the rest of the day off," said May.

"Why don't you come with me? I have some shopping to do in Sharpville. Barons doesn't have the makeup I use. The stuff carried here makes me break out," said Brenda.

"I don't know," said May. "I was looking forward to going home and taking a long soak."

"You can take a soak when you get back. It won't take long. It's only twenty-five miles and we can stop at Danny's and get something to eat when we start back," Brenda encouraged. "Besides, I need the company. I hate driving by myself."

"Okay, why not?" said May. "At least I know I won't run into Carlson in Sharpville." Brenda laughed and took her arm to guide the way to where her car was parked.

The girls enjoyed the trip. They sang along with the radio, and May could feel herself relaxing. This had been a good idea, she thought. They shopped in the drug store, and Brenda waved and spoke to several people she recognized. She shopped there often to get her makeup.

After shopping, they headed to Danny's to get a burger. They waved and spoke to Danny, who was behind the counter.

"Hi, girls," said Danny. "What can I get for you?"

"We want a couple of your delicious burgers, Danny," said Brenda.

"Okay, just take a seat. I'll send them out in a few minutes. Do you want drinks?"

"I'll take iced tea," said May.

"Me, too," agreed Brenda. "I'm driving." She grinned at Danny, and the girls went to find a table. It was not crowded. It was early evening and the dinner crowd had not begun to arrive yet. They picked a table midways of the room and sat down to wait. The waitress brought them their iced teas and told them the burgers would be there shortly.

Brenda stood up. "While we are waiting on our burgers, I am going to take a quick look in the magic mirror." She went over to the magic mirror and sat in the chair in front of it. May followed along with her. May had heard of the magic mirror, but she had never looked in it before.

Brenda sat looking in the mirror, but she only saw her reflection. She sighed and rose. "Nothing, I have never seen anyone. I am beginning to think there is no true love for me," said Brenda. She turned and looked at May. "You have to try," she said.

May was wary, but she sat in the chair. When she looked in the magic mirror, she gasped.

"Silas," she whispered.

Silas looked into the mirror in front of him. He had been washing his face. Silas started grinning. "Well, if it isn't my woodland sprite," he said. May flushed. She had not known Silas was aware of her spying on him all of those years ago. "You know my name?" asked Silas.

"Yes," nodded May.

"What's your name?" he asked.

"May Merril,"

"Are you in Rolling Fork?" asked Silas.

"No, my family moved away from Rolling Fork ten years ago," said May. "We moved to Barons."

"Where's Barons?" asked Silas frowning.

"It is twenty-five miles South of Sharpville," said May.

"They have a magic mirror, too?" asked Silas.

"Yes, it's in Danny's Bar and Grill," said May.

Silas smiled at May. "You are my true love," he said. "You are not married, are you?" he asked.

May flushed. "No, are you?"

"No, I was waiting for my woodland sprite to come back," he said.

"Are you still on the reservation?" asked May.

"Yes, Jamie and I help out with security and deliver large loads for the lumber yard. You remember Jamie?"

"Yes, I remember Jamie," said May.

"Don't run off before I can get to you. I will see you as soon as I can make arrangements to be away," said Silas. "Don't forget me."

"If I haven't forgotten you in ten years, I don't think you have anything to worry about," said May smiling. The mirror faded to her reflection.

Brenda had been standing beside May watching and listening in amazement as May carried on a conversation with the magic mirror.

"You really saw someone in the mirror?" asked Brenda.

"Yes, I did. Not just any someone, but someone I had a

huge crush on ten years ago. I didn't know he had even seen me. He said he is coming to find me," said May excitedly.

The waitress had brought their burgers and was standing listening to their conversation with a huge smile on her face. "Congratulations, the magic mirror has been silent a lot lately. We were beginning to think it had quit working. It's good to know it was just waiting for the right person to sit in front of it," The waitress took their burgers to their table and then hurried off to spread the word about the magic mirror working.

When May and Brenda were ready to leave, they went to the counter to pay for their burgers. "They are on the house," said Danny. "The magic mirror says so."

"Thank you," said May and Brenda with big smiles. They waved as they left.

The trip home was filled with excitement. Brenda seemed to be almost as excited as May.

"It really works," said Brenda. "I just have to keep trying, and maybe I will see someone."

"When we get home, I would appreciate it if you would not say anything about me seeing Silas in the mirror. I don't want my family to know about it yet," said May.

Brenda shook her head. "You would think they would be happy for you."

"They want me to marry Carlson. He has been working on them. I told him no and I refused to go out with him, but I can't convince him or my family it is not going to happen," said May.

"Won't your family be happy you have found your true love?" asked Brenda.

"No, all they are going to see is he is Indian. They are going to be against us being together. One of the reasons they were happy to move away from Rolling Fork was because it was so close to the reservation. They will be thinking up all kinds of reasons why we can't be together." May shuddered.

"Don't worry, I won't say anything, but they are going to find out when he shows up in town," said Brenda.

"Maybe I can convince him to elope," said May.

Brenda shook her head. "I think you should put your foot down. You are twenty-five years old, and they have no right to tell you how to live your life."

"I know you are right," said May. "I need to stand up to them and stop them from bossing me around. After all, if they cared about me at all, they would stop pushing me to marry Carlson, when I have told them repeatedly I can't stand the man. He gives me the creeps."

Brenda laughed. "You should have quit that job ages ago," she said.

"It's not so easy to find a job in a town as small as Barons," said May.

Brenda pulled into a parking space in front of May's apartment. May started to get out and then turned back to Brenda.

"Thanks for talking me into going with you today," she said.

"Thanks for going with me. I haven't had this much fun in ages. You be sure to introduce me to Silas before you two take off," said Brenda.

"I will," promised May. She hurried into her apartment.

May entered her apartment and locked her door. She lay down her purchases and stood for a minute, smiling into space. Then she started dancing around laughing.

"I saw Silas. He's coming for me," she said.

May dropped down on her couch and leaned back. She leaned back and closed her eyes. Her eyes popped back open, and she jumped back up and went to run a bath. "A nice long soak is just what I need," she said.

~

Silas had left the bathroom where he had gone to wash his face. He went into his living room and pulled out his laptop computer. He pulled up a map search and looked for Barons. As soon as he found it, he printed instructions on how to get there from the reservation. He studied the directions and smiled, laying them down on the table, going to pack a bag. His woodland sprite was waiting for him, and he did not plan on keeping her waiting long.

Silas picked up his phone and called Jamie. "Jamie," he said when Jamie answered. "I am going to be gone for a few days, maybe a week. Can you get someone to help you while I am gone?"

"Yeah, Tim Little Eagle is not doing anything. He'll help out. Where are you going?" asked Jamie.

"I'm going to Barons. I have to find my true love. She saw me in a magic mirror in Sharpville," said Silas.

"What!" exclaimed Jamie. "I can come with you."

"I can handle it. Besides, we have several loads to deliver," said Silas.

He and Jamie ran a business together. They contracted to use their trucks to make large deliveries. The lumber yard, partly owned by their dad, was one of their best customers, and they were contracted to make a delivery the next day.

"I can get someone else to make the delivery," said Jamie.

"No, I will be fine. You need to be here to keep an eye on things," said Silas.

"Okay," sighed Jamie. "But, if you need me, just call."

"I will," promised Silas. "I have to go. I'm going to take my car. If you need to use my truck, help yourself. You have a key. Keep a check on my house while I'm gone."

"Okay, call me when you get there and, Silas, good luck," said Jamie.

Silas smiled. "Thanks."

He hung up his phone and took his suitcase out to his car. He went back and turned out the lights and locked up his house. Silas climbed into his car with a smile of satisfaction. He was on his way. He did not get far before he saw Moon Walking on the side of the street. She motioned for him to stop, so he pulled over next to her and lowered his window.

"Hello, Moon Walking, can I help you?" he asked.

"No, I just wanted to wish you a safe journey to find your true love. It is always good to follow love's memory, but be careful. Watch out for outside forces trying to interfere," she said.

"Thanks, I will be careful," said Silas.

Moon Walking moved back and waved him on. Silas waved back and, putting up his window, resumed his journey. Moon Walking's blessing meant a lot to him.

CHAPTER 2

May went in to work the next morning in a good mood. She was smiling and happy. Everyone who saw her stopped and looked twice. They were not used to May being so bubbly. Even Carlson did a double-take. He wondered if May was warming up to his pursuit. May was oblivious to them all. She was only conscious of Silas and how long it would be until he arrived.

"I wish I had given him my phone number," she thought. She managed to do her work and was leaving for her lunch break. Brenda had called and wanted to meet her for lunch.

Silas had driven through the night with stops for gas and coffee. He had been on the road for over twelve hours and was getting close to his destination. He drove into the town of Barons at a few minutes after twelve. He was driving down the main street when he saw May come out of an office and start to walk down the street. He quickly parked his car and got out.

"May," he called. May stopped at the sound of her name and turned around to see who was calling her. She saw Silas hurrying toward her.

"Silas," she said. She started going to him. She was walking fast at first, then faster, and then they were running toward each other. Silas opened his arms and May ran into them. They closed around her tightly. She was hugging him just as tight. Then they were kissing. They ignored everyone around and devoured each other. People were stopping and staring. They were not used to anyone kissing in the middle of town on the street.

Brenda was coming down the street to meet May. When she saw what was happening, she started grinning. "Silas has arrived," she said. "Wow."

Even Carlson was watching from the window of his office. He stormed out of his office and over to May and Silas. "What is the meaning of this, May? Why are you kissing this person? What about us?"

May drew back slightly from Silas. Without even looking at Carlson she sighed and smiled at Silas. "Buzz off, Carlson. There is no us, there never has been and there never will be." She raised her face for another kiss. Carlson turned and went back to his office when he heard several snickers because of May's answer.

Brenda was close enough to hear May's remarks to Carlson. She laughed. "You go, girl," she said.

May heard her and reluctantly pulled back from Silas. She smiled up at Silas. "You came," she said.

"Of course, I had to find my woodland sprite," he said, smiling at her.

"Wow," said Brenda. "You two are going to melt the sidewalk. Are there any more like you at home?" she asked inquiringly.

Silas smiled at her briefly and then looked back at May. "Yes, I have a brother, Jamie," he said.

"How do I meet him?" asked Brenda.

Silas looked only at May as he answered Brenda. "Maybe you could attend our wedding. Jamie will be there." May grinned at him.

"Aren't you moving a little fast?" asked Brenda.

"Fast," echoed Silas. "It has been ten years. I would say we have to make up for lost time."

"Yes," agreed May.

"Where can we be alone?" asked Silas.

May became aware of the audience they had gathered. She smiled at everyone. "We can go to my apartment," said May.

Just then, a police car pulled to a stop next to the curb. It was a deputy sheriff's car. May groaned when her brother Gunner exited the car. He looked in astonishment to see his sister in the arms of a man he had never seen before. "What's going on here, May?" He looked at Silas. "Who are you?"

"Gunner, this is Silas. I've known him for ten years, and I'm going to marry him, so you had better treat him right," May said.

Gunner and Silas looked at her and smiled.

"May Flower Merril, what's come over you?" inquired Gunner.

"May Flower, I like it," said Silas with a grin.

"Gunner Merril, I'm going to murder you. It took me forever to get people to stop calling me May Flower," said May.

Gunner laughed. "You better watch it, May Flower. It's against the law to threaten a police officer."

"I didn't threaten a police officer. I threatened my obnoxious big brother."

"He's your brother?" asked Silas.

"Yes, this is my brother, Gunner," said May.

"It's nice to meet you, Gunner," said Silas holding out his hand.

Gunner shook his hand and looked at him hard. "If you two have known each other for ten years, how come we have never met?" asked Gunner.

"She was only a child at the time. Then your family moved away. "I only found out where she was yesterday when May saw me in the magic mirror. I came as fast as I could," replied Silas.

"You saw him in the magic mirror in Sharpville?" asked Gunner.

May nodded her head. "Brenda and I went to Sharpville yesterday. We stopped at Danny's on the way home. I was astonished when I saw Silas after all of this time," said May. May smiled up at Silas. "I was also very happy."

Silas squeezed her hand. "So was I," he said.

"Do Mom and Dad know?" asked Gunner.

"No," May frowned. "I'll tell them later. Right now, I'm going to enjoy some time with Silas."

"Okay," said Gunner with a shrug. "I wouldn't go home. It will be the first place they look for you." He took out his keys and handed her his apartment key. "You can go to my place." May took the key and reached up and kissed Gunner on the cheek.

She took Silas' hand and started toward the car she had seen him get out of. They got into the car and drove off.

Brenda was left standing on the sidewalk with Gunner. "Well, there goes my lunch date," said Brenda.

Gunner looked at her. "I'm on my lunch break. You want to join me?"

"Do I get to ride in the police car?" asked Brenda.

Gunner laughed. "No, the restaurant is just a few steps away. We can walk."

"Sure," agreed Brenda following along with Gunner.

"Maybe next time," said Gunner.

"What?" asked Brenda.

"Maybe next time I'll let you ride in my police car," said Gunner as he held the door open for her.

Brenda smiled up at him. "I'll look forward to it." They went on inside.

May and Silas had just walked into Gunner's apartment when her phone rang. May answered it without looking to see who it was. "Hello."

"What's this I hear about you standing out in the middle of town kissing some stranger?" demanded Violet Merril.

"Mother," said May with a groan.

"Yes, Mother, explain yourself, young lady."

"No, I will not explain myself. I am twenty-five years old, and who I kiss is none of your business. You lost the right to talk to me about kissing when you tried to force me to marry Carlson Welks," said May.

May hung up the phone and turned it off. She looked at Silas and smiled. He was looking at her with approval. "Does your family always give you such a hard time?" asked Silas.

May nodded. "I don't know why they act the way they do. It's like they all know something I don't know, and they are determined to keep me from finding out what it is."

Silas pulled her into his arms and kissed her again. She moaned when he raised his head and looked down at her. "You are so beautiful, my woodland sprite. How I have missed you," said Silas.

"Why do you call me a woodland sprite?" asked May looking up into his eyes.

"Because I did not know your name and I always saw you in the woods," said Silas.

"I never told anyone about seeing you except Dancing Eagle. He was an old Indian man who lived on our farm close to the woods. I used to go see him in his shack and take him food. We would sit and talk," said May.

"I remember Dancing Eagle. He died a few years ago," said Silas.

"My folks don't know I overheard them talking once, but Dancing Eagle owned the farm we were living on. He was a distant cousin of my mother's. My dad would not let her talk about it. He was ashamed to have to take help. When he couldn't make it on the farm, he jumped at the chance to leave it. He was offered a job in the lumber yard here in Barons."

May took Silas' hand and led him to the sofa. They sat down and she leaned against him, and he held her close in his arms. He continued to place kisses around on her face while she talked. He managed to kiss her on the lips a few times. May was busy scattering kisses also. Silas lifted her up and settled her into his lap. He was determined to be as close as possible.

May leaned back against Silas and looked up at him. "When are we going to be married?" she asked.

"I would marry you today if I could," said Silas. "Jamie would never forgive me if he was not at my wedding."

"Well, why don't we just call Jamie? We could grab Brenda and have Jamie meet us in Vegas," said May.

Silas frowned and looked down at May. "You want to elope?" he asked.

May looked up at Silas. "I take it by your reaction, you are not in favor of eloping," said May.

Silas tightened his arms around May. It was as if he thought he had to hold on to her or she would slip away from him. "If you want to elope, we can elope to the reservation.

We can be married quickly there, and all of my family and friends would wish us well," said Silas.

"I never thought about being married on the reservation," said May

"Would you not want to be married on the reservation?" asked Silas.

May touched her hands to his face and looked into his eyes. "I have nothing against being married on the reservation, I just had not thought about it. I think it would be nice to be around people who wish us well, just because they like us. Unlike my family, they will not be in favor of us being married anywhere," said May.

"I do not know your family, except for Gunner. He seems like a nice guy," said Silas.

"He is a nice guy. My mother, Violet, and my sister, Autumn, work in the Golden Locks hair salon. Autumn never has an opinion of her own. She parrots Mother. Mother told her to marry Serin Whiticar and she obediently did so. She has two boys. Serin works at a corner store and gas station. My sister, April, is in college. She has avoided Mother's match-making so far. Dad works at the lumber yard. He is the only person Mother ever listens to. She still manages to get him to see things her way most of the time. Gunner escaped her clutches. He moved out when he got the Deputy Sheriff's job. I think she was afraid to bother him. Maybe she was afraid he would give her a parking ticket or something. I don't know. I just know she leaves him alone."

May took a deep breath and looked at Silas. He had been listening quietly. "There you have it — my family in a nutshell. You ready to run for the hills, now?" she asked.

"Now, why would I want to run for the hills? You are not your family. I have been waiting for you for a long time, and I am not about to let anyone come between us. We will handle all disputes together. We are going to be one. Moon Walking assured me of this before I started on this journey. I love you, my woodland sprite. I will always love you."

"I love you, too. I have since I was fifteen," said May.

He pulled her closer and kissed her deeply.

They were interrupted by a knock at the door. "Do you think they found us?" asked May. She did not move from Silas' lap. She frowned at the door. The knock sounded again. "I guess I had better see who it is," said May, reluctantly getting up from Silas' lap.

She opened the door and saw a complete stranger standing there.

"Can I help you?" she asked.

"May Flower Merril?" he asked.

"Yes," answered May. "What do you want?"

"I'm Chad Brown from the law firm of Brown and Sons. Your brother told me where to find you. May I come in?"

"Yeah, sure," said May standing back and holding the door open for him. Silas had stood and was still in front of the sofa. "This is my fiancé Silas Light Feather," said May smiling at Silas. She sure liked saying that. "Mr. Brown, why did my brother send you to me?" asked May after Mr. Brown had shaken Silas' hand.

"I went to the Sheriff's office to try and locate you and I ran into your brother. When I explained who I was and why I wanted to see you, he sent me here."

"Why don't you explain it to me?" said May.

Mr. Brown opened his briefcase and removed some papers. Among them was a letter. "Miss Merril, my firm represented the late Dancing Eagle. He left you this letter and his estate. He left instructions for it to be delivered when you turned twenty-five. We had a little trouble locating you," said Mr. Brown.

He handed the letter to May and waited for her to open and read it. May took a deep breath and opened the letter. Her eyes became misty as she saw the familiar writing of Dancing Eagle. May blinked her eyes and held tightly to Silas' hand as she started to read the letter.

My sweet May Flower,

I have missed seeing your lovely face since your parents took you away. I enjoyed having you visit me and talk to me. I hope you manage to get together with young Light Feather. I have checked him out, and he is a good man and will take care of you. I have left you my place and money. I have money in an account to take care of the place until you are twenty-five. I didn't want to have it turned over to you before then, because I was afraid your parents would force you to sell it if they found out about it before you were old enough to stand up to them. The land is just outside of the reservation. It is on the northern corner and close to the mine. The semi-precious stones found in the mine continue onto the property for quite a ways. I never wanted to mine it. I did not need the money, and I did not want to have all of the strangers on my property. Be guided by young Light Feather in your decisions about this matter. You can trust him. Beware of false advice from others who want what you have. I love you like a daughter. You made an old man's days brighter. Be happy.

Dancing Eagle

May looked up at Silas. He had been reading along with her over her shoulder. "He left me his place. He said you were meant for me," said May, blinking away her tears.

Silas pulled her close and hugged her. He was feeling a little teary-eyed himself. He was honored to know Dancing Eagle thought so highly of him.

Mr. Brown cleared his throat. He had been sitting quietly, waiting for them to finish the letter. "I have the papers transferring the ownership of the property to May Flower Merril. If you will just sign these papers, I will have the new title registered, and you will take possession of your inheritance. The papers will explain everything to you," said Mr. Brown.

May and Silas took the papers and looked them over. May signed the ones Mr. Brown pointed out and kept a copy for herself. She would look them over more after Mr. Brown was gone.

"Enjoy your inheritance, Miss Merril," said Mr. Brown. He shook hands with May and Silas.

They walked him to the door and closed it behind him. May turned and went into Silas' arms. "Dancing Eagle didn't forget me," she whispered.

"You are not forgettable," said Silas, hugging her close.

May leaned back and looked into his eyes.

"Dancing Eagle would be so pleased we are together," she said with a smile.

"Yes, he would," agreed Silas.

"Are you going to tell your family?" asked Silas.

"Just Gunner for now. Dancing Eagle was right. They would have tried to make me sell the place. I would have fought them, but they might have found a way to get around me to get what they wanted. I'm glad he waited. We will figure it all out later. Where were we when we were inter-rupted?" May asked.

"I think I can find where we left off," said Silas.

There wasn't much talking going on after he started kissing her, and she was all in favor of no talking.

CHAPTER 3

Gunner let himself into his apartment at six, after he finished his shift. He had knocked first, but when there was no answer, he opened the door with his spare key and entered. He stopped and smiled when he saw May and Silas sound asleep on his sofa. They were stretched out in each others arms. May was laying half on Silas.

Gunner quietly went on through to his bedroom. He took a shower and started to gather clothes to wear the next day. He thought about it and stopped. He went into the kitchen and made himself a sandwich. After getting a drink, he took both into his bedroom and softly closed the door. After sitting the drink on his bedside table, he sat on the side of the bed and turned the TV on. He lowered the sound and leaned back on his bed to eat his sandwich and watch the news.

After he finished the sandwich, he switched channels, trying to find something interesting to watch. He settled on a boxing match, but it had just started when his phone rang. He muted the sound on the TV and answered the phone quickly before it could wake May and Silas.

"Hello," he said quietly.

"Gunner," demanded his mother in a strident voice. "Have you talked to May? She's not answering her phone, and she is not at her apartment."

"No, I haven't talked to May tonight," said Gunner with a grin. "Why are you looking for her?"

"I was trying to talk to her earlier, and she hung up on me. She must have turned her phone off because it goes straight to voice mail. I have to stop her before she does something stupid." Violet was getting more agitated the longer she talked.

Gunner had a big grin on his face. "Your idea of stupid may not be May's idea of stupid," said Gunner.

"For her to squander her inheritance and run off with a stranger is my idea of stupid," said Violet.

Gunner frowned. "What do you know about her inheritance?" asked Gunner.

"I found out a year ago when someone from the law firm was trying to locate May before her birthday," said Violet.

"So you thought you could marry her off to Carlson Welks and the two of you would conspire to take her inheritance." Gunner paused. He was furious with his mother.

"It wasn't like that," protested Violet. "We just wanted to be sure May was protected."

"Yeah, right," said Gunner. "I wondered why such a creep as Carlson suddenly showed an interest in marrying May. It was all your doing. You didn't care about May's happiness. You didn't care if she was miserable. All you thought about was getting your greedy hands on her inheritance." Gunner was furious with his mother.

"I was trying to help," protested Violet.

"Trying to help yourself," said Gunner. "I don't want to talk to you anymore right now. You leave May alone. If you try to mess with her inheritance, I will file charges against you myself." Gunner hung up the phone. He looked back at the TV, but he was too mad to pay attention to a boxing match.

He turned off his phone and looked up. May and Silas were standing in the door looking at him. May smiled. "We heard you talking to Mother," she said.

"I'm sorry you heard me go off on her. She just makes me so mad with her twisted logic," said Gunner.

May went over to the bed. She held onto Silas' hand so he had to go with her. She sat on the side of the bed. Gunner scooted over so she would have more room. "I don't blame you for getting mad at her. I must admit I couldn't understand why she and Carlson wanted me to marry him so bad. I knew he didn't care about me, but I couldn't figure out what was in it for him and Mother. It was all about Dancing Eagle's land and money. She may have known about the mine, too," said May.

"What mine?" asked Gunner.

"There is a mine on the reservation. It produces semi-precious stones. The gems are on Dancing Eagle's land also. He was never interested in mining them. I don't know if Mother knew about them. Dancing Eagle wrote me a letter. He said he waited until my twenty-fifth birthday to give me my inheritance because he wanted to protect me from Mother. He was afraid she would try to take it away from me," May stopped and looked at Gunner. "He was right," she said.

Silas hugged her shoulder and Gunner squeezed her hand. "You don't have to worry about Mother. Silas and I are here to look after you," said Gunner.

May smiled up at him. Her eyes were misty.

"Have you guys decided what you are doing next?" asked Gunner.

"We are going to get another day's rest and pack up May's things," said Silas.

"We are going to the reservation. We will be married there. I hoped you would come and bring Brenda with you," said May.

"I'll be there. You'll have to talk to Brenda. I'll be glad to bring her with me. Just tell me when," said Gunner.

May leaned forward and hugged him. "Thanks for being such a great big brother," said May.

"So, you are not still plotting to murder me, May Flower?" asked Gunner with a laugh. He was trying to lighten the atmosphere.

"No, I'll even let you get away with calling me May Flower," said May with a smile.

"Have you guys had anything to eat?" asked Gunner.

"I raided your refrigerator earlier and made us some sandwiches," said May.

"How about we order a pizza?" asked Gunner. "Do you feel like celebrating your engagement with pizza?"

"I would love to celebrate our engagement with pizza," said May, standing and looking up at Silas with love. Silas hugged her and agreed.

Gunner sat up and grabbed his phone to order a pizza. "What do you want on it?" he asked.

"Everything," said May.

Gunner laughed. "Anything you don't like on your pizza?" he asked Silas.

"No, I can eat anything as long as it is on a pizza," said Silas.

Gunner and May laughed. "You are the perfect man for my little sister," said Gunner.

"I could have told you that," said May with a smile at Silas.

Gunner called for a pizza to be delivered while May went in search of her phone.

When she turned on her phone, she laughed at all the missed calls and messages from her mother. She quickly deleted all of the messages without reading or listening to them. She punched in Brenda's phone number.

"Hey, Girl, have you surfaced?" asked Brenda.

May laughed. "Yes, for a while. I had my phone off so I wouldn't have to talk to my mother. Silas and I are going to pack my things tomorrow and head to the reservation the next day. We are going to be married on the reservation. Gunner is going to come, and I would love if you could come,"

"I don't know if I can take time off and be able to afford a trip right now," said Brenda.

"Gunner will be driving, and he said you could come with him," said May.

"He did. Ask him if he is going in his patrol car," said Brenda.

May turned around to look at Gunner. He was talking with Silas. "Brenda wanted to know if you are going in your patrol car," said May.

Gunner laughed. "Tell her, no, not this time," he said.

May looked curious but shook her head. "He said no, not this time," said May.

"Shucks, tell him I would love to ride with him. Thank him for me," said Brenda.

"Okay, I'll talk to you later. I think I hear our pizza delivery," said May. May hung up and turned her phone back off. "Brenda said she would love to ride with you. She said to tell you thank you," May told Gunner.

There was a knock at the door and Gunner went to get their pizza. May went to the kitchen to get plates and she directed Silas to get out drinks. They had the plates and drinks on the table and ready when Gunner brought the pizza into the kitchen.

"Ummm, it smells great," said May. Gunner and Silas both smiled at her. She didn't care. She loved pizza. May put two slices on each plate and passed them around.

"Are there any pizza places on the reservation?' asked May.

"Yes, there are two," laughed Silas. "If there wasn't, I would have to see about opening one as much as you like pizza."

May leaned over and kissed him. "I would take you over pizza any day," said May.

"There you have it," said Gunner. "If I find a girl who will take me over pizza, I will be ready to claim her." They all laughed.

"It may be hard to do," said May with a laugh. "After all, you are getting on up there in age," teased May.

"Watch it," teased Silas. "Gunner and I are close to the same age."

Gunner laughed at the look on May's face. "Alright, I'll stop teasing if you two are going to team up on me," said May with a smile at both of them.

After they finished the pizza and cleaned up the kitchen, May and Silas got ready to leave. They had decided to go to May's apartment. They were hoping her mother had given up on trying to find her.

"You are welcome to stay here," said Gunner. "If you see Mother or anyone else you know when you get there, turn around and come back. I don't want your last days here filled with fighting," said Gunner.

"Okay," agreed May. "If I see anyone, I'll come back. Thanks for helping. I love you."

"I love you, too. I just want you to be happy. I think Silas is the one to make you happy," said Gunner.

"He is," agreed May with a loving look at Silas.

Silas gave Gunner a reassuring smile and handshake before he and May headed for her apartment.

Gunner watched them leave from his front door. "There should be some way to protect them from Violet," he thought. Maybe he could talk his dad into helping. It was worth a try. He closed the door and went inside. He took his phone and called his dad.

"Hello," answered Guy Merril.

"Hi, Dad, this is Gunner."

"I guess you want to talk about your mother," said Guy.

"Yes, I do. Is there any way you can keep her from harassing May?" asked Gunner.

"She just wants what is best for May. Your mother didn't want to see her end up on the farm by the reservation," said Guy.

"Mother couldn't care less about where May ends up. She just conspired with Carlson to try and steal her inheritance from her before she found out about it. If she had been looking out for May, she would have told the lawyers where May was a year ago when they came looking for her. Instead, she pretended she didn't know where to find her and tried to force her into a marriage with that jerk Carlson Welks. She didn't care about May saying 'no.' She kept pushing. It was all to get a hold of May's inheritance," said Gunner.

Guy sighed. "You have it all wrong, son."

"You are not going to try and stop her, are you? You are going to stand back and let her continue to try to force May into a situation she doesn't deserve to have to put up with," said Gunner with disgust. "Well, you can tell Mother to back off. I am helping May and her young man. If Mother interferes, I will bring the law down on her big time. You tell her she doesn't want to mess with me."

Gunner hung up his phone in disgust. The way things

were going, he might decide to move back to Rolling Fork with May. He didn't have any family here to worry about. At least there he would be close to May. Maybe they could talk April into moving there when she was done with college. He could check it out when he went to the wedding.

May and Silas slipped into her apartment and quickly closed and locked the door. They went around and closed all of the shades before turning on the lights. Silas looked around at May's apartment. It was attractively decorated.

May took his hand and led him over to the sofa. "I rented the apartment furnished. It won't take long to pack my stuff," she said, looking around.

"Maybe I should have brought my truck," said Silas.

"If I have too much, I can store it with Gunner and he can bring it with him when he comes to the wedding," said May. Silas took her into his arms and kissed her. "I have a large bed in the next room," said May between kisses. "It would be much more comfortable than the sofa."

Silas groaned. "I am trying to be a gentleman and not rush you."

May took his face in her hands and looked into his eyes. "I have been waiting for this moment for ten years. I refuse to wait any longer for someone to say a few words. They can say all the words they want to later. I want to be with you now. Make me fly like the eagle. Dancing Eagle would approve." May kissed him hungrily. Silas kissed her just as fiercely. May took his hand and showed him the way to the bedroom.

They turned off the lights off so no one would disturb them.

CHAPTER 4

The first thing May did after making breakfast the next morning was to get Silas to take her by the law office so she could write her resignation and hand it to Carlson. Carlson stuttered a bit but he accepted her letter. She cleaned out her desk and stopped to talk to the head of secretaries.

"I have been training Nina for a while. She will do a good job if you keep an eye on her and let her build up her confidence," said May.

"I'll keep an eye on her," promised Jo. "Good luck."

"Thank you," said May. "I won't need luck. I have Silas." She smiled and waved at Silas, who was waiting for her by the door.

May hurried over to him and let him take her box of things she had removed from her desk. They stopped to pick up a few boxes and then headed for the apartment. May wrapped and packed her kitchen things. She didn't have a lot. She had not been in the habit of having company except for Brenda. She had a few pictures and statues. She had them packed, and Silas placed the boxes in the front room as fast as she packed them. She cleared the bathroom except for what she would need to use before leaving the next morning.

She got out her suitcases and packed her clothes, leaving out an outfit for traveling. She packed all of her towels, except one, and bed linen, except what was on the bed. Since they were staying another night, the sheets on the bed would have to be packed in the morning.

Silas started taking some of her things out and seeing what he could fit in the trunk of his car.

He was a very good organizer and fit almost all of her things in the trunk. He placed one of her suitcases, her laptop, and her TV in the back seat. He fitted the seat belt around the TV so it would not move. He left the floor behind the front seat open for the last minute additions in the morning. The few things left for morning would be easy to fit in there. He made room on the back seat for a small cooler to keep their drinks cold.

"Do you have a car?" asked Silas.

May laughed. "Yeah, I am going to give the keys and title to Gunner and let him sell it for me. If I need one later, I'll get one in Rolling Fork."

"Since my car is packed, why don't we take your car and go out to eat. We can pick up some snacks and drinks for the trip," said Silas.

"Okay, I can go by and talk to Gunner about selling my car while we are out," said May.

They met Gunner in front of the apartment as they were leaving. May explained about the car, and he told her to take the car and park it at his apartment. He could take them out to eat and shop. "You can give me your car keys now and I'll come by in the morning and pick up your apartment keys. I'll hand them in and tell your landlord you are leaving," said Gunner.

"Thanks," agreed May. "I hadn't even thought about the apartment keys."

They took May's car and parked it at Gunner's. May handed him the keys to the car. "I really appreciate this," she said.

"It is no problem. I think I know someone who is looking for a car," said Gunner.

They spotted Brenda as they were on their way to eat. Gunner stopped and asked her to join them. Brenda seemed happy to climb into the car with them. May looked between Gunner and Brenda curiously. They looked attracted to each other. May smiled but didn't say anything. She leaned against Silas and smiled at him happily.

Silas hugged her close and looked at her lovingly. What a wonderful gift the Great Spirit and the magic mirror had sent his way, he thought.

Gunner chose the restaurant, and they entered and claimed a booth. May and Silas sat on one side and Brenda and Gunner on the other. They laughed and chatted while enjoying their meal and the company. Everyone was relaxed and having a good time.

"Aunt May! Aunt May!" exclaimed two young boys as they spotted May in the booth.

Autumn's husband was there with their boys, Stan and Gus. Silas moved out of the booth, so May could get up and hug the boys. After they had hugged May, they spotted Gunner and had to hug him as well.

"Where's Autumn?" asked May.

"She went to your folk's house. I thought I would give the boys a treat and get them over being disappointed for not going to visit with their mom," said Serin.

"Why didn't she take them with her?" asked Gunner."

"I don't know," shrugged Serin. "She said something about her mother calling her and took off."

"Let's move to a larger table so you all can join us," said Gunner.

"Serin, this is my fiancé Silas Light Feather. Silas, this is my sister's husband Serin Whiticar and the two munchkins are Stan and Gus," said May.

"It's nice to meet you all," said Silas, holding out his hand for Serin to shake.

"It's nice to meet you," said Serin, shaking his hand.

Gunner had managed to attract the waitress's attention and she was moving them to a larger table and taking Serin and the boys' orders.

Stan and Gus looked at Silas curiously.

"How did you get a name like Light Feather?" asked Stan.

"It is an Indian name. I am an Indian," Silas replied.

"Cool," said both boys grinning.

May smiled up at Silas. "Yeah, cool," she echoed.

"How did you and Silas meet?" asked Serin curiously.

"We met ten years ago when my family lived next to the Indian Reservation," said May.

"Does your mother know?" asked Serin.

"Oh, yeah, it's probably why she called Autumn over," said May.

"Probably," agreed Serin.

"Well, I wish you luck. I hope you will be very happy," said Serin.

"Thank you," said May and Silas.

The waitress brought the food and topped up all of their drinks. They settled back to watch the boys enjoy their night out. When they finished eating, they all walked out together, after Gunner insisted on paying the check. The boys gave May and Gunner more hugs. They even hugged Silas. He was surprised but was used to dealing with youngsters on the reservation, so he returned their hugs happily. Serin gave May a hug and shook Silas' hand again before putting his boys in their car seats and leaving. The boys continued to wave as they left. Everyone waved back at them.

"I'm going to miss those boys," said May.

"Maybe they will be allowed to visit us when they are a little older," suggested Silas.

May looked at him and grinned. "Maybe," she agreed.

Gunner dropped May and Silas at her apartment. Brenda got out and hugged May and promised she would see her at the wedding.

"Don't you get married without me," said Brenda.

"I won't," said May.

She and Silas waved goodbye to Brenda and Gunner before turning and entering the apartment.

"Do you want to take a shower tonight or wait until morning?" asked May.

"Tonight, so we have time to share. If we wait until morning, we will be in a hurry," said Silas, drawing her into his arms.

"Good, we have to share the towel, too. I only left one unpacked," said May.

Silas laughed. "I don't mind sharing with you," he whispered in her ear.

May smiled and, taking his hand, led him toward the bathroom.

They were up and had the remainder of things packed in the car and were ready to leave when Gunner pulled into the parking lot. He got out, and May handed him her apartment keys and the signed title to the car. He gave May a hug and shook Silas' hand.

"You take care of my little sister," he said to Silas.

"I promise to take very good care of her. She is my life," assured Silas.

"Give me a call when you arrive," said Gunner.

"We will," promised May.

"Be careful. I will see you at the wedding. Let me know your plans as soon as possible so I can make arrangements here," said Gunner.

"We will. You take care of yourself," said May, giving him another hug.

Silas opened her door so she could settle into her seat for the long journey. May waved through the window at Gunner as Silas went around the car and started the engine. They all waved as Gunner watched them pull into the road and leave.

Gunner sighed and went to his car to take May's apartment keys and turn them in. When Gunner went into the manager's office and explained about May's leaving, the manager took one look at Gunner's Deputy Sheriff's badge and accepted the keys with no protest. Gunner smiled as he left. Sometimes the badge came in handy. He returned to his car and headed into work. He met his friend Carl as he was approaching the front door.

"Hey, Carl, are you still looking for a good used car?" asked Gunner.

"Yeah, you heard of anything?" asked Carl.

"My sister May has left town to be married, and she left her car with me to sell. If you are interested, it's at my place. You could stop by after work and look it over," suggested Gunner.

"Thanks, I'll be there," said Carl. He hurried to join his partner to go on patrol.

Gunner went inside and went into the Sheriff's office. He paused in front of the desk and waited for the Sheriff to look up at him. The Sheriff looked up. "What can I do for you, Gunner?" he asked.

My sister May is getting married, and I want to put in for the next two months off. I have more than two months of vacation time accumulated," said Gunner when it looked like the Sheriff was going to protest.

The Sheriff sighed. "I am going to approve it this time, but next time try to give us a little more notice."

Gunner grinned. "Yes, Sir." He turned and left the office with a satisfied look on his face.

With two months free time, I will have plenty of time to look around Rolling Fork, thought Gunner.

He saw Brenda walking down the sidewalk on her way to work. He pulled up to the curb and waved at her. Brenda came over to his car and smiled at him. "Did May and Silas get away okay?" she asked.

"Yes, they are on their way. The reason I called you over was to talk about our trip to the wedding."

"You haven't changed your mind about me going with you, have you?" she asked.

"No, nothing like that, I am going to take a couple of months off so I can have a good look around while I am there. I didn't know how you would feel about extending your stay," Gunner paused expectantly.

"I don't know," said Brenda. "Let me check at work and get back to you. When are you thinking about going?"

"As soon as I hear from May and Silas," said Gunner.

"Okay, I'll call you tonight," said Brenda. She waved and left for work. Her mind was not really on work. She was thinking about two months of time to convince Gunner how perfect they would be together. She had been aware of her feelings for Gunner for a while, but Gunner had acted as if he was unaware of her existence. Maybe now he would notice how well they suited each other.

Little did she know, Gunner was very aware of her existence. He had been for some time, but he had thought she was interested in someone else. Now, he knew she was available and he would have two months to convince her he was who she was looking for. Gunner smiled. The future was looking good.

Gunner headed for his apartment. Carl had stopped and was looking at May's car. Gunner parked and went over to join him. He took the keys out and unlocked the door. Carl grinned. "I'm on my break. I thought as long as I was close by, I would stop and see what the car looked like."

"It is in good shape. May didn't drive it a lot. Everything is so close in town. You can walk just about anywhere you want to go," said Gunner.

"How much is she asking for it?" asked Carl.

"Five thousand dollars," said Gunner. "You want to take it for a spin?"

Carl looked at his watch. "Just a quick one," he agreed.

Gunner handed him the keys and stood back so he could drive it. Carl drove around the block and pulled back into the parking space in front of Gunner's apartment.

"It runs smooth," said Carl. "I'll run by the bank and pick up the cash. The title place stays open late. I'll meet you there after work."

"Okay," agreed Gunner. He had May's signed title ready to be transferred. He would have to be sure and wear his uniform to the title place. There was less chance of a problem if he was in uniform.

Carl met Gunner at the title place after work. He handed over the envelope of money, and Gunner gave him the signed title. They went inside and had the car transferred to Carl, and Gunner handed him the keys.

"Thanks," said Carl with a big grin.

Carl was riding with his partner. They followed Gunner back to his apartment so Carl could pick up his new car. Carl was very pleased with his purchase.

Gunner went inside to wait for a call from May and Silas. He knew it would be a while yet before they arrived. It was a long trip. He would feel better when he heard they had arrived.

The phone rang when he entered his apartment. "Hello," said Gunner.

"Hi, big brother, what's this I hear about May ruining her life," asked April.

Gunner laughed. "I guess Mother called you."

"Yes, she called. I know not to believe anything she says, but she was very upset," said April.

"She is only upset because we found her out before she could get her hands on May's inheritance," said Gunner.

"What inheritance?" asked April.

"May inherited a place in Rolling Fork from Dancing Eagle," said Gunner.

"Dancing Eagle, you mean the old Indian whose place we used to live on?' asked April.

"Yes, it turns out, Dancing Eagle was worth quite a bit, and he left it all to May. He stipulated she couldn't inherit until she turned twenty-five. He wanted to keep Mother from taking it away from May."

April laughed. "It sounds like he knew Mother pretty well," said April. "Where's May now?"

Gunner laughed. "She's on her way to Rolling Fork with her fiancé, Silas Light Feather. She knew him when she was fifteen. When she saw him in the magic mirror in Danny's, he lost no time in looking her up."

"Things sure happen fast when I'm not around," said April.

"They are very much in love and are planning on being married on the reservation. I'm going to the wedding and I was planning on calling you to see if you could make it."

"When is it going to be?" asked April.

"They are going to let me know as soon as they get there and make arrangements," said Gunner.

"Well, as soon as you find out, call me and I will see if I can get time away," said April

"Okay," said Gunner. "Don't pay any attention to Mother. I have never seen May so happy."

"Okay, I love you, big brother," said April.

"I love you, too, shortcakes," said Gunner.

April laughed at the familiar name Gunner had called her because she liked pancakes so much.

CHAPTER 5

*I*t was still daylight when May and Silas were on the road going into Rolling Fork. Silas pointed to the land they were passing. "We are passing your land. Do you want to stop and take a quick look at the house?" asked Silas.

"If you are not too tired from driving, or we can wait until tomorrow," said May.

"It won't take long, and I don't know what jobs Jamie has set up for tomorrow," said Silas

He turned into the drive and followed it to the house. May and Silas looked around in astonishment. The house looked great. It was in good shape and freshly painted. The grounds around the house were freshly cut, and a flower garden was growing to one side.

Silas helped May out of the car, and they stood looking around for a minute before heading for the house. They went up on the porch and looked at the porch swing at one end.

"I don't remember a porch swing when we lived here," said May.

They went over and tried the door. It opened easily. A

table was just inside the front door. There were two house keys in a bowl and a letter beside it.

"You don't think someone could be living here?" asked May.

Silas picked up the letter and looked at it.

"Why don't you read the letter? It's addressed to you. Maybe it will explain things," he said holding the letter out to May.

May took the letter and looked at her name on it. It said, "May Flower." May shook her head as she opened the letter. It looked like she was going to be May Flower again whether she liked it or not.

May Flower,

Welcome to your home. My friend Dancing Eagle asked me to look after the place and keep it ready for you. He wanted to be sure you and Young Light Feather had a good impression of the place. I have had people from the reservation to look after the house and to keep up with the yard work.

Dancing Eagle had Glen Black Feather draw up the papers to incorporate your land into the reservation. It will still be your land, but you would not have to pay any inheritance taxes on it. You need to talk to Glen Black Feather to get all of the details.

Your land borders the Black Feather property. The young Black Feather boys are raising horses. If you don't want to farm your land, Dancing Eagle thought you might lease part of it to them for raising horses. You can discuss all of this with Glen Black Feather.

I have been looking forward to your arrival and will enjoy watching as you and Young Light Feather add your offspring to our community.

-Moon Walking

"Wow," said May. "I'm keeping this as a souvenir. A letter from Moon Walking."

Silas laughed. He had been reading along with May. "I wonder if we will always be young boys to her," he said.

"I wonder how many offspring she is talking about," said May.

Silas laughed again and hugged May. "Let's have a look around," he suggested.

They went on into the living room. It was furnished with a sofa and two rocking chairs. There were several tables around. One was in front of the sofa. There was a table in between the rocking chairs. Another table against the wall would work great for her TV. There was a large round woven rug in front of the sofa. There was a fireplace in one corner of the room.

They went on into the kitchen. It had a small area to one side. There was a table and six chairs there. It had a stove and refrigerator. There was even a microwave above the stove. There was a door leading off the kitchen. It led to a small room with a washer and dryer. There were shelves. They had some canned goods and household supplies stored on the shelves. They went back into the kitchen and looked in the refrigerator.

"Wow," said May. "When Moon Walking gets a house prepared, she doesn't miss a thing."

Silas smiled. "Moon Walking never misses anything."

They started down the hall leading from the kitchen. The first door led to a bathroom. May took a quick look and went on down the hall. The next two doors opened into bedrooms. They had double beds and chests in them. The last room opened into a larger bedroom. It had a large bed and a dresser and a chest. There was a big walk-in closet and a bathroom leading from the bedroom.

"Do you want to stay here?" asked Silas.

"Only if you stay with me," said May.

"Of course I'll stay with you. We have everything we need for tonight," said Silas.

"I would love to spend the night in our new home in your arms," said May hugging Silas.

Silas kissed her. "I'll go unload the car while you call Gunner," he said.

He kissed her one more time and headed for the door. May took out her phone. She had a big smile on her face as she dialed Gunner's number.

"Hello," said Gunner.

"Hello, big brother, we made it. I am standing in the living room of my new home. It's beautiful," said May.

"You stopped at your house?" asked Gunner.

"Yes, it's in great shape. Dancing Eagle had asked Moon Walking to take care of it for me. And when I say she took care, I mean she took care. She even had the refrigerator stocked. You're going to love it. It has three bedrooms, so you'll have somewhere to stay when you come to the wedding."

Gunner laughed. "It sounds like you are becoming fond of the place," he said.

"I love the place," said May.

"Where is Silas?" asked Gunner

"Silas is unloading the car now," said May. "He'll be in soon.

"I have good news. I sold your car. It sold for five thousand dollars. I'll bring the money with me when I come to the wedding. Have you made any plans?

"We just got here. We haven't even talked to anyone but you. Thanks for handling the car for me. I really wasn't expecting it to be sold so fast or for so much," said May.

"You're welcome. I also had a call from April. She said she will try to come to the wedding," said Gunner.

"Let me guess, Mother called her," said May.

Gunner laughed. "You got it. I explained things to her. She understands now."

"Thanks, Gunner, I really appreciate everything you have done to help," said May.

"That's what big brothers are for," replied Gunner.

"Well, I lucked up and got a great one," said May. "I'll let you know what's happening as soon as I know." They hung up, and May went to see if she could help Silas.

Silas had already taken the boxes from her kitchen into her new kitchen. He sat the other boxes on the table in the dining nook.

He was taking her suitcases into the bedroom when she went looking for him. May went out to the car with him and got her laptop while he took out the TV. May went ahead and opened and held the door so he could carry the TV into the living room. He sat the TV on the table in the living room, but he didn't try to hook it up. They decided to wait until the next day to work with it. May took her laptop into the bedroom and laid it on the dresser. May went to see what she could fix them to eat while Silas called Jamie to let him know he had returned.

"Hello," said Jamie.

"May and I are here," said Silas.

"Are you at your place?" asked Jamie.

"No, we stopped at May's house. We will stay here tonight and come to the reservation in the morning."

"May has a place?" asked Jamie.

43

"Yes, Dancing Eagle left his place to her," said Silas.

"Dancing Eagle has been gone for a while. Is the house livable?" asked Jamie.

"Yes, Moon Walking has been looking after it," said Silas.

Jamie laughed. "I'm sure it's in great shape. Moon Walking would accept no less.

"I will see you tomorrow and tell you all about it. All I want to do tonight is eat and rest," said Silas.

"Okay, I'll see you tomorrow."

They both hung up, and Silas went to see what May had prepared to eat.

May had prepared a large omelet and halved it, putting it on two plates and adding toast and water. She smiled at Silas when he joined her in the kitchen.

"It smells good," said Silas. "It looks good, too."

"I wanted something quick. If you are as tired as I am, I know you are ready for some sleep," said May.

Silas grinned as he sat down to enjoy his meal. "We will sleep as soon as we break in the bed," said Silas with a smile.

May laughed. "Are you sure you are not too tired?"

"I will never be too tired to make love with you," he declared.

"I will hold you to that," said May giving his hand a squeeze.

They finished their meal, washed the dishes, locked the doors, and turned out the lights. They were both very happy to be home.

The next morning, after eating and cleaning the kitchen, they headed for Silas' place on the reservation. He had a small one-bedroom house. He had lived there for several years, but he realized it would not do to raise a family. May's place would be much better. Silas packed some more of his clothes so he would have more to choose from. He took his bags and put them in the trunk of his car. He decided to take May by to talk with Glen Black Feather before going to find Jamie.

Silas escorted May into Glen's office and knocked on his inner door. There was no one at the desk out front.

"Come in," said Glen.

"Hi, Uncle Glen," said Silas. May looked at Silas curiously. Silas had not mentioned Glen was his uncle.

"Hello, Silas," said Glen, rising to meet them. "This must be May Flower Merril."

"Yes," said Silas.

"It's nice to meet you, Miss Merril," said Glen, holding his hand out for a handshake.

"Please, call me May," said May.

"Alright, May. Dancing Eagle was very fond of you. He talked about you a lot. He was sure you and Silas would be together someday," remarked Glen.

"He was right," said May.

"I'm glad to hear it," said Glen. "Are you familiar with how Dancing Eagle set up your inheritance?"

"I've read the papers the lawyer gave me," said May.

"Good," said Glen.

"Dancing Eagle filled out a request to have your land incorporated into the reservation. He would not have been able to do this if you had not been part Indian. Since Dancing Eagle was your cousin through your mother, you are Indian, so he was able to get his application approved. The property is still yours, but you can not sell it to anyone who is not Indian. You also would have to get the Elder's permission to sell," explained Glen.

"I don't want to sell," said May.

"Dancing Eagle also thought you might want to lease part of the land," said Glen. "He also mentioned the mine. He thought you could make a deal with the miners, similar to what my family made. They would work the mine and pay you a monthly fee."

"How does that work?" asked May.

"The Black Feather family receives a monthly check. It is a share of the profits from the mine. It is divided between each of my children and one share to my wife and myself. One share goes to the reservation to help with whatever it needs. If you wanted to make a similar deal, you could have part of your money put aside to be divided between your future children," said Glen.

May looked at Silas and smiled. He smiled back at her, but he did not say anything. "I think I would like to have money put aside for my children," said May. "I also would like to have trust funds set up for my sister's boys, Stan and Gus Whiticar, with each of them getting a share. Could you handle talking to the mining company and the Elders and setting it up for me?" asked May.

"Yes, I can handle it, but are you sure you don't want to wait and think about it first?" asked Glen. He glanced at Silas.

"It is fine, Uncle Glen. Whatever May wants to do. I like the idea of our future children having college funds waiting for them," laughed Silas. He looked at May and smiled. She smiled back and nodded her agreement.

"Do you think your sons would be interested in leasing some of my land for their horses?" asked May.

"I'll ask them and let you know," said Glen. "I need to get your phone number so I can reach you."

"Yes, of course," said May as she gave him her number.

"Where are you two headed next?" asked Glen, leaning back in his chair and smiling at them.

"I'm going to show May around and take her to meet Jamie and my folks," said Silas.

Glen stood and held out his hand to May and Silas. "Tell

my sister we are looking forward to a visit from her," said Glen.

"I will tell her, but you know she does not get out much," said Silas.

"Myla came to Mark and Doris's wedding, and we haven't heard from her since. Daisy has been busy helping with the new babies and she hasn't checked up on her. I'll be sure to let Daisy know she needs to see Myla," said Glen.

"Thanks, Uncle Glen," said Silas.

Silas and May said goodbye and went outside.

CHAPTER 6

S ilas drove to the lumber yard and stopped in front of the office.

"Why are we stopping at the lumber yard?" asked May.

"Jamie is here. He is waiting to take a load to deliver it. My dad is also here. He is one of the owners," said Silas.

"Oh," said May, getting out as Silas opened her door. Silas put an arm around her and guided toward the door of the office.

Jamie and Tim Little Eagle rose from their seats when Silas and May entered. Jamie had a big smile on his face as he came forward to give May a hug. May hugged him back with a smile.

"Welcome, I am glad Silas has found his love." Jamie leaned back and looked at her and then turned to Silas. "You are very lucky, my brother. I am very happy for you both. You have brought me a sister."

Silas smiled and pulled May close to his side. "May, this is my brother, Jamie, and our friend Tim Little Eagle," said Silas.

"It's nice to meet you both," said May with a smile.

Tim smiled and came forward and shook her hand.

The inner office door opened, and Adam Long Feather entered the room. He started smiling when he saw Silas was there. "Silas, you made it back," said Adam.

"Dad, this is May. She and I will be married as soon as I can make the arrangements," said Silas. "May, this is my Dad, Adam Long Feather."

"I'm very pleased to meet you, Sir," said May.

Adam came forward and hugged May. "Call me Adam. Welcome to our family. I have always wanted a daughter. Your mother will be very happy," said Adam to Silas. "Are you going out to see her?" asked Adam.

"We will go to see Mom as soon as I check with Little Bear to see when we can be married. We have to let May's brother know when it's going to be so he can come," said Silas. "Maybe we can come out for supper. Do you think it will be alright with, Mom?"

"I'll call your mom and see how she's doing. I will call you and let you know what she says," said Adam.

"Okay," said Silas.

"Could we see Moon Walking?" asked May. "I need to thank her for looking after my place."

"We can try. We will have to see if we can find her. She stays busy," said Silas.

"Okay," agreed May.

Silas and May said goodbye to his Dad and started outside. Jamie followed them out. Silas had his arm around May and guided her to the passenger side of his car.

"When are you planning on coming back to work?" asked Jamie.

"I'll let you know tonight," said Silas.

"Okay," agreed Jamie. "Welcome to our family, little sister."

"Thank you, Jamie. I can't wait for you to meet Gunner," said May with a smile. "I think you two will be friends."

"Who is Gunner?" asked Jamie.

"Gunner is May's brother. He's a great guy," said Silas. May smiled up at Silas, silently thanking him for his words.

"I'll look forward to meeting him," said Jamie.

"We will see you tonight," said Silas as he seated May in the car and went to the driver's side and entered. Jamie waved to them and turned to go back inside.

Silas drove downtown and showed May around. He drove by the school and the sports complex. They drove by the building used for a community center. As they drove by the community center, Silas spotted Moon Walking coming out of the building. Silas turned his car around and drove back coming to a stop beside Moon Walking.

Moon Walking smiled at them and waited patiently for them to exit the car and come over to her. "Welcome home, May Flower," said Moon Walking.

"Thank you," said May. "Thank you for taking such good care of Dancing Eagle's place. It was a joy to come home and feel so welcome."

"Dancing Eagle was my friend. He talked about you a lot. I think he missed your cookies," said Moon Walking, smiling.

May laughed. "He had a sweet tooth. While my mother was at work at the hair salon in Rolling Fork, I used to bake cookies. I always saved some to take to Dancing Eagle. He loved them," remarked May to Silas and Moon Walking.

"Yes, he missed those treats when your family moved you away," agreed Moon Walking.

"I missed my talks with him. He was a great storyteller," said May.

"Yes, he was," agreed Moon Walking. She looked at Silas.

"I have reserved the community center for your wedding one week from today. I have talked to Little Bear, and he will be available. Some of the ladies will decorate the building, and Smiling Fawn will make a cake, and there will be others making other refreshments. I have put the Black Feather boys in charge of bringing drinks," said Moon Walking. May just stood there with a look of amazement on her face.

Silas smiled. "Thank you, Moon Walking. You have arranged everything perfectly."

"Yes, you have," agreed May. "Thank You."

"I want you to be happy here. Also, it was important for your brother and sister to like it here," said Moon Walking. "I will see you later." Moon Walking turned and went back inside the building.

May glanced at Silas. "It looked like she came out just to talk to us," she said.

"She probably did," said Silas with a shrug.

"I wonder what she meant about Gunner and April," said May.

"I guess we will have to wait and see, but if Moon Walking thinks it's important for them to be happy here, it is important."

"I guess so," agreed May. "Well, do you want to go see your mom?"

"Sure, I should tell you, before we go to see her, about her. She gets nervous around a lot of people. She is very shy and doesn't do well in crowds. She is usually alright when she is at home with us. When she gets to know you as part of our family, she will be okay around you. I just wanted to warn you, she may be a little quiet at first, but she will come to love you," said Silas.

May put her hands on his face and looked in his eyes. "Don't worry, your mom and I will work it out," said May.

"I love you," said Silas, kissing her before helping her into the car and starting for his childhood home.

Silas pulled up in front of his family home and stopped. May sat looking at the house while Silas went around to open her door.

"It's a lovely home, but isn't it a little big?" asked May.

"My dad is part owner of a lumber yard," said Silas. "The house started out small. He would add on to it as it was needed. He added rooms for me and Jamie. He built a small apartment at the back for Lone Wolf and his wife Rosa. They take care of things and keep an eye on Mom. Dad did not want to leave her out here by herself while he was working. Rosa does the cooking and Lone Wolf takes care of the yard," Silas explained as he led her up onto the porch.

Silas did not knock. He opened the door and looked around. "Where is everybody?" called Silas.

"Silas, your dad called to tell me you were coming, but I thought you would be later," said Rosa as she hurried into the room.

"We were going to be later, but Moon Walking took care of our errands, so we came on out," said Silas. "Rosa, this is May. She and I are going to be married. May, meet Rosa, she is my second mom," said Silas.

Rosa grinned at Silas. "It's good to see this one settle down with such a lovely person," said Rosa.

"Thank you, Rosa," aid May.

"Where's Mom?" asked Silas.

"She's out back in the garden with her sketchbook," said Rosa.

Silas started through the kitchen to the back door. As he

passed Rosa, he leaned down and kissed her cheek. Rosa smiled at him and waved him on.

They went out the back door into a small, but lovely garden. There were flowers blooming everywhere. Silas led her to the center of the garden, where a small gazebo sat. Myla Long Feather sat with a sketchbook absorbed in drawing a scene from the garden.

"Hello, Mom," said Silas quietly.

Myla looked up and smiled a beautiful smile at Silas and May. "This must be May Flower," said Myla.

Silas looked surprised. "Yes, it is, How did you know?" asked Silas.

"Moon Walking came by a few days ago. She said you had gone to pick up your bride, a relative of Dancing Eagle. She seemed very pleased," said Myla.

"Yes, she is. Mom, this is May. May, meet my Mom, Myla."

May came forward and took Myla's hand. "I am very happy to meet you, Myla," she said. She leaned forward and gave Myla a hug. Myla smiled and hugged her back. Silas watched in amazement. He had never seen his Mom take to anyone so fast.

He and May sat down on a nearby bench and chatted with Myla while waiting for Adam and Jamie to get there. "Our wedding is set for a week from today. It is going to be at the community center," said Silas.

"Yes, Dear, I know. Moon Walking told me," said Myla. "I told her I would help decorate the community center."

Silas stared at his mom. She was more relaxed than he had seen her in a long time. He hoped it would last until after the wedding.

"My brother, Gunner, and my sister, April, will be coming to the wedding," said May.

"I will look forward to meeting them," said Myla. "Do they need somewhere to stay while they are here?" asked Myla.

"No, Dancing Eagle's house has plenty of room," said May.

"If you find you need more room, we will be happy to have them stay here. You are family, now. We would be glad to help," said Myla.

"I will remember," said May. "Thank you so much for offering."

"Your garden is beautiful," said May looking around.

"Yes, Lone Wolf has a way with flowers. He can make them grow when everyone else is moaning about theirs not growing," said Myla laughing.

Adam and Jamie came into the garden. They stopped in astonishment when they heard Myla laughing with May. Adam came on over and leaned in and gave Myla a kiss,

"Hello, Dear, I see you have met May," said Adam. Jamie came over and kissed her cheek, also.

"Yes," said Myla smiling. "We have been getting to know each other. I think Silas is very lucky."

May smiled at Myla. "Thank you, but I am the lucky one. I get to join this lovely family and be with the love of my life. After all, the magic mirror says Silas is my one true love." Silas squeezed her hand and Myla smiled at her happily.

"You can't argue with the magic mirror," said Jamie. "I wish it would send someone my way."

"Be patient, dear. Your time is coming. Moon Walking told me so," said Myla

"Moon Walking told you," repeated Jamie.

Silas laughed. "Be careful what you wish for."

"It is fine," said Jamie. "It's just I will be looking at every girl I see wondering if she is the one." Everyone laughed at Jamie's disgruntled expression.

"Don't try so hard to find her," said Myla. "Relax and let her find you."

"Did Moon Walking say anything else?" asked Jamie.

"She said it will happen like a bolt of lightning," said Myla, smiling at Jamie.

"Okay, are we expecting rain?" asked Jamie looking at the sky. They all laughed again.

"Supper is ready," called Rosa from the back door.

"We'll be right there, Rosa," answered Adam.

He went to Myla and took her hand to help her up. When she rose from her seat, her sketch pad fell to the ground. May reached down to pick it up for her. It had opened to a page, and May glanced at the picture showing. She gasped.

"It's me," she said, looking at the picture. Silas, Adam, and Jamie all crowded around to see the picture. They were astonished to see May looking back at them from the page of Myla's sketch pad.

"I hope you don't mind," said Myla. "I drew it from a dream I had a few days ago. It seemed important to get the picture drawn. At the time, I didn't know why. Now, I know it was because you are my son's chosen and my daughter."

"You were ready to meet May before you saw her," said Silas.

"Yes," agreed Myla with a majestic nod. "I felt like I already knew her. When she walked into the garden with Silas, I breathed a sigh of relief that she was finally here."

May went over and hugged Myla. Myla hugged her back. When they drew apart, both had wet eyelashes. The guys were not exactly dry-eyed.

They all laughed and headed once more for the door and Rosa, who was standing at the door waiting for them with a big smile on her face. Adam and Myla went in first. Silas and May were next. Jamie came in last and, leaning down, kissed Rosa on her cheek as he passed her. Rosa smiled at him and closed the door behind him.

Adam held the chair to his right and waited for Myla to sit. He took the chair at the head of the table for himself. Silas seated May at Adam's left and seated himself next to her. Jamie went to sit next to Myla. Lone Wolf sat at the foot of the table and Rosa sat next to Jamie.

May looked curiously at the plates of food on the table and glanced at Silas. "Have you ever had taco salad?" asked Silas.

"No," said May, shaking her head.

"Well you start like this," he said. He took a handful of tortilla chips and crushed them in the center of his plate. "Next, you put shredded lettuce on the chips, over the lettuce you add cut up pieces of tomato. The meat sauce is put over the tomato, then shredded cheese is put on top."

May had been copying him as he went along, and when he finished, she took a bite from her plate.

"Oh, this is good," exclaimed May, taking another bite.

Everyone had been watching Silas and May. When she spoke, they laughed and started fixing their own plates.

"This is a favorite meal for Jamie and me," said Silas. "We were always begging Rosa to make it for us."

"I can see why. It's great," said May.

When they finished their taco salad, Silas and Jamie helped Rosa bring in the desert. It was hot apple pie with vanilla ice cream topping it. Rosa sliced it and put it on plates. Jamie put scoops of ice cream on each slice, and Silas brought the plates to the table and passed them around.

May looked at the desert and her mouth watered. She waited for everyone to get their dessert before taking a bite, but it was hard to wait. It smelled so good. She gave Silas a big smile when he sat down beside her and picked up his fork. It was the signal she had been waiting for. She dug in.

"Ummm," said May. She immediately took another bite and savored.

"Rosa, this is great. Are there any more cooks in your family looking for work?" asked May.

Rosa smiled. "My granddaughter is looking for work. I taught her how to cook. I won't say she's as good as me, but she's close." Rosa laughed. Everyone joined in with the laughter.

"Do you mean Shala?" asked Silas.

"Yes, she has finished school and is eager to be on her own away from her dad's supervision," said Rosa.

"Would she want to live in?" asked May.

"She would prefer to live in, but could try coming in daily to see how it works out," said Rosa.

May smiled at Rosa. "I would love for her to live in after the wedding, but until then, I am going to have a house full of friends and relatives," said May.

"I was thinking," said Silas, "maybe Gunner would like to use my house while he is here. He could still spend all of the time he wants to with us, but would have more freedom to come and go."

"I think that is a great idea," said May. "I'll ask him and see what he thinks about it."

"Would you ask Shala to come and see me, Rosa?" asked May.

"Yes, I will. May I give her your phone number so she can call you and arrange a time?" asked Rosa.

"Sure," said May, and she gave her number to Rosa. She noticed Myla writing the number in her sketch pad at the same time.

May smiled. "You may call me anytime. I will love hearing from you," she told Myla. Myla smiled back at her and nodded.

Lone Wolf, sitting at the end of the table, had been eating very quietly; now, he smiled and nodded in satisfaction as he gazed around at everyone.

CHAPTER 7

*R*osa wouldn't let them help with cleanup, so shortly after supper, May and Silas hugged Myla and Adam. May even hugged Jamie while Silas shook his hand. With promises to call, they headed for home.

When they arrived at home, May and Silas stood on the porch and looked at the stars. Silas had his arms around May, holding her close to him while she stood in front of him looking up. May sighed. "It is so beautiful," she said. "I never knew I could be so happy." She turned in his arms and looked up at him. "I love you so much, Silas Long Feather," she whispered.

Silas leaned forward and kissed her. May snuggled closer and kissed him back. When they came up for air, he continued to hold her close.

"I thank the Great Spirit every day for sending you into my life. I love you now and forever, my woodland sprite."

He started kissing her again, and May tightened her arms around him as if she would never let go.

The next morning, Silas left his car for May to use and went to work in his truck. They had stopped to get the truck the night before on their way home. After Silas left for work, May called Gunner.

"Hello, little sister," said Gunner.

"Hi, Gunner. Moon Walking has arranged for the wedding to be a week from yesterday. Will you be able to make it?" asked May.

"Yes, I have already taken time off so I can stay awhile and look around. I will call Brenda and see if she can make it," said Gunner.

"Silas had an idea. He has a one-bedroom house on the reservation. He is staying here with me, so he thought you might like to use it while you are here. It would give you more freedom to look around. What do you think?" asked May.

"Tell Silas I accept. It's a great idea. I love the idea of getting out and looking around," said Gunner. "I will call April and Brenda and let them know when the wedding is. If there is anything I can do to help, let me know."

"You can walk me down the aisle," said May.

"I would love to walk you down the aisle. Are you sure you wouldn't rather have Dad?" asked Gunner.

"No, I want you. You don't have to dress in a suit. The Indian wedding is less formal. Just wear a nice dress shirt and some slacks," said May.

"Okay. I am sure I already have what I need. Stay happy, May Flower," said Gunner. "I love you, and I think you picked a winner to be my new brother." May wiped her eyelashes where tears had gathered. "I'll let you know when to expect us," said Gunner.

"Okay," agreed May as she hung up the phone.

Before she could do anything else, there was a knock at the door. May turned to open it. She was surprised to see three women outside the door. They were all smiling at her, so she smiled back.

"Hello," said the older one. "I'm Daisy Black Feather. Moon Walking has asked us to help get the Community Center ready for your wedding. So, we decided we would come over and welcome you and introduce ourselves. These are my daughters-in-law, Doris and Willow."

"It's nice to meet you. I'm May Flower Merril. Please, come in."

May stood back and motioned them inside.

"Please have a seat," said May. "Would you like some coffee or tea?"

"No, thank you, we can't stay long," said Daisy. "We just wanted to welcome you to the reservation and our family."

"Thank you," said May. "I am so glad you stopped by." May had a big smile for Camille, who was in Willow's arms. "She's beautiful," said May.

"Thank you," said Willow.

"My other daughter-in-law, Glenda, would have come with us, but her baby was fussy, so she decided to keep him home," said Daisy.

"It will be nice to enlarge our group of friends on the reservation," said Doris.

"Yes," agreed Willow. "Our group is growing."

"With new wives and new babies, it is great," agreed Daisy with a smile.

"It sounds like it," agreed May with a smile. She was still eyeing Camille with longing.

"Would you like to hold her?" asked Willow.

"I would love to," said May as she rose and took Camille in her arms. She bounced her in her arms and talked baby talk to her. The other three women just smiled. They understood perfectly. New babies just begged to be held and loved.

The door opened and Silas came in. He stopped short when he saw May holding Camille in her arms. He started grinning. He looked around at the others. "Hello, everyone, it's nice to see you, but I have to go. I forgot my phone and I'm on my way to Rolling Fork with a load," he explained to May. "I thought I'd make a quick stop and pick it up." He gave May a quick kiss, waved goodbye to the others and grabbed his phone on the way out the door.

Daisy laughed. "He probably forgot his phone on purpose so he would have an excuse to stop," said Daisy with a laugh.

"I think I distracted him when he was leaving," said May with a smile.

Doris and Willow laughed. "You have to learn to put his phone with his keys. He can't go anywhere without his keys, so he will automatically pick up his phone," said Doris.

"Good idea," agreed May with a smile.

May noticed the armbands on Willow and Doris. She leaned over for a closer look. "Those look nice," said May.

"Thanks," said both ladies.

"These are marriage bracelets. I made one for Mark and he made this one for me. We exchanged them at our wedding ceremony. They were blessed by Derrick Little Bear when he performed the ceremony," said Doris.

"You exchange them instead of rings?" asked May.

"Some people do, but we had both. It's up to the couple what they want to do," said Doris.

May looked thoughtful while she studied the bracelet. "Silas hasn't said anything about them," she said. "Are they hard to make?"

"I could show you how to make it, if you want to," said Doris.

"I'll ask Silas tonight and let you know," said May.

"You would have to start soon and do a simple design. You have less than a week," reminded Doris.

"I'll let you know tomorrow," said May.

Camille started to get fussy, and Willow got up to take her.

"We should go," said Daisy. "It's time for Camille's bottle. Let us know if there is anything we can do to help."

"Thank you all for coming by," said May. "I love having friends and family around."

She got up and followed the ladies out and watched as Willow strapped Camille into her seat and got into the back seat with her. Daisy and Doris got into the front, with Doris driving. They waved as they backed up and pulled away. May waved back and smiled at them.

Silas and Jamie were on their way to Rolling Fork with a load of building supplies. Jamie had laughed when Silas had asked him to stop on the way to pick up his phone. When they had stopped in front of the house and Jamie had seen Doris's car parked out front, he had decided to wait in the truck.

"We have to deliver this load before lunch, and if I go in, we will be delayed longer," said Jamie.

Silas had hurried out to get his phone. He had expected to see Doris, but he had not expected to see his Aunt Daisy and Willow. He also had not expected the thrill he had experienced when he had seen May holding the baby and looking so natural doing it. He could imagine how wonderful it would be to see her holding their child.

Silas had a goofy grin on his face when he returned to the truck. Jamie looked at him and grinned.

"Is Doris doing okay?" asked Jamie.

"She looked okay," said Silas. "Aunt Daisy and Willow were there too. Willow had Camille with her."

Jamie shook his head. "They probably were there to help with wedding things," said Jamie.

"I guess," agreed Silas. "I have been so busy, I haven't

bought May a ring, yet. Do you think we will have time to go by the jewelers in Rolling Fork and see what they have?"

"Sure, as soon as we are unloaded, we can go shopping," agreed Jamie. "Are you and May going to make wedding bracelets?" asked Jamie.

"I haven't thought about it," said Silas looking thoughtful.

"They would have to be simple. You don't have a lot of time," said Jamie.

"I'll have to talk to May tonight and see if she wants to make one," said Silas. "Maybe I should buy the makings while I am in Rolling Fork, just in case she wants to make one."

Jamie shrugged. "It won't hurt to be prepared. If you don't use them maybe, I can when I find my true love," said Jamie with a grin.

Silas smiled at him. "I haven't heard the weather report today, but I don't think we are expecting a thunderstorm."

Jamie groaned. "Why can't Moon Walking come right out and tell us what she means."

Silas laughed. "What's the fun in that? Moon Walking has to keep us guessing. She wants to keep us on our toes."

"I suppose," agreed Jamie. "I sure hope she is right."

"Moon Walking is always right," said Silas. "What happens may not always be what we are expecting, but she is always right."

"Yeah, I know," agreed Jamie. He grinned at Silas. "At least I know there is hope. All I have to do is wait and pray for rain." Silas burst out laughing and Jamie joined in.

Jamie and Silas delivered their load in plenty of time. As soon as it was unloaded, they went shopping. They went first into a craft store to find the supplies for the bracelets. Silas bought a variety of different colored beads, leather straps, needles and thread, and strings to tie the bracelets on with. Since he did not know what would be needed, he decided more was better. He hoped he had what would be needed.

After they left the craft store, they wandered around looking for a jewelry store. An antique store caught Silas' eye, and he decided to go in and look around. Jamie followed him in. He was curious about Silas going in, but he didn't say anything.

Silas could not have explained why he went in either. He had felt a pull as he went by and knew he was supposed to go in. A short, older man came in from a back room.

"Hello, gentlemen, how are you today?" he asked.

"We are fine," answered Jamie.

"Is there anything in particular you are looking for today?" asked the man.

Silas stopped suddenly and then walked forward to the display of rings in a glass case. He was looking at one ring in particular. It was a square cut emerald surrounded by small diamonds in an antique setting.

Silas pointed at the ring. "Could I see this ring?" he asked.

The man unlocked the case and brought out the ring Silas indicated.

Silas looked at it and knew he had to get this ring for May. "How much is it?" asked Silas.

The man grinned. "You are in luck. It is half price today. Moon Walking and I had an agreement. If you came by today and asked for this ring, it was to be half price. It also has wedding rings to match."

Silas and Jamie looked at him in amazement.

"When did Moon Walking come in?" asked Jamie.

"She came by two days ago," said the man grinning. "She always stops for a visit and a cup of tea when she comes to Rolling Fork."

"I'll take them," said Silas.

"How do you know if they will fit?" asked Jamie.

Silas looked at him. "They will fit. Moon Walking picked them out," he said.

"Oh, yeah," agreed Jamie.

Silas put the rings into his pocket and patted them with satisfaction. They were perfect for May. After all, the emerald was her birthstone.

Jamie looked over at him and grinned. He was pleased to see Silas so happy.

"Do you want to stop for a burger?" asked Jamie.

"If you are buying," agreed Silas. "I'm a little short at the moment."

"It's on me," agreed Jamie with a laugh. "The ring will be perfect for May. I think she will love it."

"I think so, too," agreed Silas. He was smiling all the way back to the lumber yard.

Silas decided to head for home as soon as they went in and let their dad know they had made it back. He was in a hurry to see May's face when she saw the ring. When he went into the house, he smelled something cooking, so he headed for the kitchen. He found May there. She had music playing while she turned fried chicken in the skillet. Silas came up behind her and, putting his arms around her, nuzzled her neck with his lips.

"Oh," said May, turning in his arms and kissing him.

"Hello," she said.

"Hello," whispered Silas around several kisses. "I missed you today."

"I missed you, too. I think I have been spoiled, having you all to myself," she said.

May pulled away and took the fried chicken out of the pan and put it on a plate. She set the plate on the table and went back into Silas' arms.

"I have something for you," said Silas.

He took the ring out of his pocket and, taking May's hand, slid the ring on her finger.

"Oh, Silas," said May holding her hand up and looking at the ring. "It's beautiful. I love it. I love you." She hugged him close and kissed him.

Silas was pleased with her reaction. He could see on her face how much she loved the ring. Moon Walking was right as usual. The ring was a perfect fit and it looked like it belonged on May's finger.

After a few more kisses, May drew back and smiled at Silas. "As much as I love my ring and you, we need to eat while things are still warm." She had already set the table before he had arrived. She had fresh rolls and mashed potatoes to go with the fried chicken. May brought the glasses of iced tea to the table and they sat down to eat.

While they were eating, May looked at Silas and smiled. "While Daisy, Doris, and Willow were here, Doris showed me her marriage bracelet. I was wondering if you would like for us to make and exchange one."

Silas started smiling. "I was thinking about the bracelets today. I went by a craft store in Rolling Fork today and picked up some supplies."

"You did!" exclaimed May.

"Yes, I don't know if we have enough time to finish them. The design would have to be very simple, but if we don't finish them in time for the wedding, we can have Derrick bless them when we finish with them," said Silas.

"I would like to try. Doris said she would help me," said May.

"Okay, I thought I could get Dad to help show me how to make it," said Silas.

May rose and went over to Silas. He pushed his chair back and she sat in his lap.

They put their arms around each other and started kissing. The food was forgotten as another hunger took over.

After a while, Silas and May managed to make it to the living room. May lay on the sofa snuggled in Silas' arms. Silas held her close and kissed the top of her head.

May stirred and looked up at Silas. "I was thinking today," she started.

Silas smiled. "What were you thinking about?" he asked.

"I didn't ask you what you would like to do about the land. I don't know if you would like to rent it or if you would like to do something with it yourself," said May.

Silas tightened his arms. "The land is yours. You can do whatever you want with it," said Silas.

"No, the land is ours. We are going to be married. We are going to live here and raise a family here. I am just going to have to get used to asking your opinion and not just making decisions by myself. I have been on my own for some time and have not had to consider anyone but myself, but I'm trying to do better. So, do you want to do something else with the land?" asked May earnestly.

"Well," said Silas considering. "I will have to think about it. I want to talk to Jamie and also I would like to see if there is a chance for Gunner to move back here. We have time. We can figure it all out later," said Silas. "Right now, I have other things on my mind." He kissed her and smiled.

May smiled back. "Anything I might be interested in?" she teased.

"I think I can interest you," said Silas kissing her and drawing her closer.

"I think you can, too," agreed May.

CHAPTER 8

*B*efore going to bed and after clearing the kitchen, Silas opened the package of bracelet supplies.

"Everything looks nice, but I have no clue about making anything with these supplies," said May.

"I know," agreed Silas. "I think we both need help."

"Let's put it all away, and I'll call Doris in the morning and see if she can give me some pointers," said May.

"I'll ask Dad for some pointers tomorrow, also. We can't work on them together. We are not supposed to show each other the bracelets until we exchange them and have them blessed," said Silas.

"Okay," agreed May with a smile. "I can keep a secret."

"Have you heard back from Gunner?" asked Silas.

"No, not since I called to tell him when the wedding was. He was going to get in touch with Brenda and April. He said he would let me know when they were on their way," said May. "He loved the idea of using your house. He said to thank you. He also said I was giving him a great new brother."

Silas smiled and looked pleased. "I'm glad he sees me as a new brother and friend, also."

"Gunner has always been surrounded by girls in our family. It's a new experience to be able to have a brother. I don't think he was ever close to Serin. He seemed to take to you right off," said May.

"Well, he is about to have a lot more males around. Jamie and I grew up close to our cousins. We all spent a lot of time together. They felt almost like brothers, and Dawn and Summer were like sisters. When we are married, Gunner will be accepted in as family."

"He will love it," said May.

"Do you remember the small house Dancing Eagle lived in?" asked Silas.

"Yes, it's not too far from here, why?" asked May.

"I was thinking about seeing if it could be fixed up so someone could use it. If we rent part of the land for horses, it would be a good place for someone to live while keeping an eye on the horses," said Silas.

May looked thoughtful. "We would have to check it out. I don't know if Moon Walking looked after it, too."

"Yeah," grinned Silas. "It will be interesting to see if she is still one step ahead of us."

"What do you mean?" asked May.

"When I went into the antique store and saw your ring. I knew it was perfect for you. The store owner said Moon Walking was in there two days ago and told him to keep the ring for me," said Silas.

"What!" exclaimed May. "I love the ring and I love you. Thank you, Moon Walking."

May heard a voice in her head answer faintly. "You are welcome." May looked around, startled.

"What's wrong?" asked Silas.

"She said, 'You are welcome,'" said May. "Can she do that?"

Silas shrugged. "With Moon Walking, anything is possible."

May snuggled closer to Silas. She was not sure how she felt about someone talking in her head.

The next morning, after Silas left for work, May was about to call Doris and let her know she was on her way when she received a call from Glen Black Feather.

"Hello, Mr. Black Feather," said May.

"Glen, please, or you can call me Uncle Glen. You are marrying Silas and you are going to be my niece," answered Glen.

"I would like that," said May. "What can I do for you, Uncle Glen?"

Glen laughed. "It's what I can do for you. I contacted the mining association. They would like to lease twenty acres of your land. They will pay fifty thousand a year until they can begin mining, then after they start extracting the jewels, you will receive a share of the profits. If you are okay with their terms, we can go ahead. They sent me a check for the first year. Are their terms okay with you?"

"They sound okay to me. What do you think?" asked May.

"It's the same deal we have with them. It has worked out okay for us. If you want to go ahead, you need to come in and sign some papers and decide how to distribute your check. If you want to set up the trust fund for your sisters' boys, you will need their social security numbers," said Glen.

"Okay, I'll call and get their numbers, and then I will come to your office. I'm going to see Doris. She is going to help me with my marriage bracelet," said May.

"Good," said Glen smiling. "I'll see you when you get here."

"Thanks, Uncle Glen," said May.

Glen chuckled as he hung up the phone. May was going to fit right into the family, he thought.

May hung up and dialed Serin.

"Hello," said Serin.

"Hello, Serin," said May. "How are the boys doing?"

"They are doing fine. How are your plans coming along?" he asked.

"They are coming along great. Our wedding is set for next Saturday. The reason I called is I need the boy's social security numbers. I'm setting up a trust fund for each of them, and my lawyer said I would need the numbers. Do you have them? I didn't want to call Autumn. I don't want Mother involved in it," May explained.

"Yes, I have them. I had to have them to take them to their doctor checkups," said Serin. He read the numbers off and May wrote them down.

"Are we invited to the wedding?" asked Serin.

"If you want to come, you will be welcome. Tell Autumn to behave herself. If she does anything to disrupt my wedding, I'll never speak to her again," said May.

"She will behave," promised Serin. "I think it is important for the boys to be there. You are a very good influence in their life. I don't want them to lose that."

"Thank you, Serin," said May smiling through misty eyes. "I'll look forward to seeing my favorite nephews, and you, too, of course. May laughed. Serin laughed, also.

They hung up, and May started for the reservation.

May entered Glen's office, and he came over and kissed her on her cheek. He took her hand and led her to a chair beside his desk.

"I have everything here for you to look over. First, do you have the boy's social security numbers?" asked Glen.

"Yes, I do," May took out the paper with the boy's

numbers and gave it to Glen. "I want their trust funds to be set up so they will receive them when they are twenty-five. I want their father to be a trustee and I was going to see if you will be their other trustee. I want it fixed so no money can be taken from their funds without both of you agreeing. They can only have money withdrawn for emergencies or for college tuition when they graduate high school. They should also be able to buy a car when they graduate. If anything happens to their father, Silas will be their other trustee. At no time will my sister have access to their trust funds."

Glen nodded and wrote down her instructions. "How much do you want to go into the boys' trust?" asked Glen.

"For this first time, I want ten thousand to go in each account. After this, they will split a share instead of getting a share each. Is there a bank on the reservation?" asked May.

"No, most of us use the bank in Rolling Fork. Derrick Bear is an officer of the bank, and he makes sure we are treated fairly," said Glen.

"Okay, we can see about setting up accounts there. I haven't transferred my money from Barons, yet. So Silas and I can open a joint account in Rolling Fork and one share can go to us. One share can go to the reservation, and the other share can be put into a trust for our future children." May paused for breath and looked at Glen.

He smiled back at her. "I can get all of this started and I'll contact Derrick Bear and have him start getting everything in order, then you and Silas can go by the bank and sign papers sometime when you are in Rolling Fork."

"Okay, I have to go and see Doris, now," said May rising. "I really want to get started on my bracelet. I don't have much time. Silas said we could wait and have Derrick bless them later if we don't finish, but it will seem to mean more if we can do it at the wedding," said May.

"I understand," said Glen. "It is a beautiful tradition. Good luck with your bracelet."

"Thank you," said May as she accepted a hug from Glen and left.

She called Silas as she started for Doris and Mark's home.

"How is my Woodland Sprite?" asked Silas.

"I am fine. I am on my way to see Doris for a lesson in bracelet making," said May.

Silas chuckled. "I have been taking instructions from my Dad."

"I just left Uncle Glen's office. He called me about the mining company. They sent fifty thousand dollars for the first year's rent on twenty acres. After they start mining, we get a share of the profits," said May. "He is going to set up accounts for us in Derrick's bank in Rolling Fork. He said we can go by and sign the papers next time we are in Rolling Fork."

"Okay, we can talk about it tonight. I don't think we have a load for them today," said Silas.

"Well, I think I have arrived. Their house is beautiful," said May.

"Yes, it is. Have fun. Don't stress out. The bracelet should be made with love. If it causes stress, it is not worth it. I love you," said Silas.

"I love you, too. I'll see you later." May hung up the phone and got out of her car. She looked around as she went toward the porch. Doris came out to greet her. An Indian man came around the corner of the house. Doris waved him off.

"It is okay, Milo. She is a relative." The man waved and kept on going.

"May looked at her curiously. "Do you have security guards?" asked May as she climbed the steps to the porch.

"Yes, my life was threatened. I think we have taken care of the problem, but Mark insists we have guards around for a while longer," said Doris. "To tell the truth, it makes me feel better to know I have someone I can call if there is trouble."

"It doesn't hurt to be sure," said May. She smiled at Doris. "Do you think you can show me how to make a bracelet?" asked May with a smile. "I have a box of things in the car, but I have no clue of how to even start."

"Let's get your things, and then we will see where we can start," said Doris.

They retrieved the materials from the car and went inside. They left the materials on the dining table while Doris gave May a quick tour of the house.

"It's a beautiful house," remarked May when they were back in the dining room.

Doris sighed. "I still can't quite believe it's mine," said Doris with a small laugh. "Mark was determined we were going to have plenty of room for my brother and sister and a growing family. I am still getting used to it."

"It won't be long before you will feel like you have lived here forever," said May with a smile.

"Maybe," agreed Doris with a shrug. "Let's see what you have here."

They opened the supplies and looked them over.

"The first thing you have to do is decide the design you want to make," said Doris. She handed May a sheet of paper and a pencil. You can draw your design on here, and then we can pick out what you need."

May accepted the pen and paper. She thought for a minute and then began to draw. She made two lines about an inch apart. At the top, she drew an I; below the I, she drew a heart, and below the heart, she drew a U. She showed it to Doris to see what she thought,

"I like it," said Doris. "It's simple but it tells the whole story. Now, you pick out your leather to make the design on."

May looked over the pieces of leather Silas had bought. There were five. One was green. One was red. One was blue. One was white, and the last one was tan. May picked the tan one.

"I think Silas would like this one best," said May.

"Okay, let's divide the beads," said Doris. "What color do you want for the I?"

"Yellow," said May.

They picked out twelve yellow beads. "You won't need but nine, but it's better to have extra in case one doesn't work," said Doris.

"We need to use red ones for the heart," said May.

They picked out some red beads and put them aside with the yellow ones.

"What about the U?" asked Doris."

"I think I'll make it green. Then I can use yellow and green down the sides," said May.

They counted out the beads and put them aside. May put the rest of the unused beads away. Doris showed her how to thread the small needle with the nylon thread. It looked like fishing line.

"You can't tie this line off. You have to weave it in," explained Doris.

She showed May what she was talking about. "See, this leather is already prepared; it has little holes to sew through," said Doris.

May took the leather and the needle and tried to copy what Doris was doing. It was harder than it looked. Doris watched as she added her first yellow bead and sewed it on. May added a second bead and looked at Doris.

Doris nodded. "You're doing great. Just make sure to weave the thread around enough to make it tight. The design will look better," said Doris.

May kept working, with Doris watching, until she finished the I. Before she started the heart, Doris took out the leather strings. They went down the sides to attach the bracelet to the arm. She showed them to May and explained how they were to be added last.

May quickly put all of her supplies away. She was preparing to go home and work on it there. She wanted to get as much done as she could while Silas was at work.

"I really appreciate you showing me how to make the bracelet," said May.

"I loved doing it," said Doris. "I also liked showing off my house. Have you bought a dress for the wedding?"

"No," said May frowning. "I need to go to Rolling Fork tomorrow. Everything is happening so fast, I seem to be behind most of the time."

"Don't worry," said Doris with a smile. "It will all get done, and then you can just sit back and enjoy married life."

"I hope so," said May.

"Call me if you run into any problems," said Doris.

"I will," assured May with a laugh. "Thanks again for helping."

She gave Doris a quick hug and hurried to her car. She put everything, including her purse with phone in it, on the back seat. Then she backed up and turned around and headed for home.

CHAPTER 9

*M*ay was driving along a few miles from her house when she saw a tree branch down in the road. She stopped her car and got out to see if she could move it. She didn't see anyone around. She slowly approached the limb. It didn't look too big. Maybe she could drag it out of the way. As May leaned down to grab a hold of the branch, she felt something hit her on the back of her head. May was stunned and fell to the ground. She blacked out for a few minutes. When she opened her eyes, she saw her car going back the way she had just come. The pain in her head was bad,

"Silas, I need you," thought May.

"May, what's wrong?" asked Silas in his mind.

"Someone hit me and stole my car," thought May.

"Are you alright?" asked Silas.

"No, I can't stay awake," said May.

"Where are you?" asked Silas.

"On the road to our house," answered May.

"Hold on, Love, I'm on my way," said Silas.

Silas was at the lumber yard. He froze when he started

talking to May in his mind. Jamie was watching him wondering what was wrong. Silas started moving toward the door and Jamie followed.

"What's wrong?" asked Jamie.

"May's hurt. Someone knocked her out and stole her car," said Silas.

"How do you know?" asked Jamie.

"She told me," answered Silas as he jumped into his truck. Jamie climbed into the passenger side, barely getting the door closed before Silas sped out of the parking lot.

"Call Mark, tell him May was attacked and the person has my car. It was headed toward Rolling Fork. Maybe they can catch him. Tell him to send an ambulance to the road leading to our home," said Silas.

Jamie took out his phone and called Mark at the Rolling Fork Police station. He was giving him the details when they spotted the branch lying in the road. They could see May next to it. She wasn't moving. Silas slammed on his brakes and put the truck in park. He jumped out and ran to May.

"May, May," he called as he knelt beside her and lifted her head. May groaned. "Come on, my Woodland Sprite, open those beautiful eyes for me," he pleaded.

Jamie was kneeling beside him.

"It looks like she was struck from behind," said Jamie. "The person was probably hiding behind the tree branch and hit her when she tried to move it out of the road."

May groaned again and tried to open her eyes. "Silas," she whispered.

"I'm right here. You are going to be alright," he said.

"My head hurts," said May.

"I know, someone hit you," said Silas.

They heard the sirens coming. There was a police car and

an ambulance. The police car stopped first, and Mark Black Feather hurried over to them.

"Is she alright?" asked Mark kneeling beside the others.

The ambulance medics were there before they could answer. They started checking May over.

"We caught the car thief. Some of the guys pulled him over as he was coming into Rolling Fork. It was Bull, from the motorcycle gang. He had escaped the mine where he was being held. If he had waited a couple of more weeks, he would have been released. Now, he going up for assault and car theft," remarked Mark.

Silas had not been paying much attention to Mark. He was watching the medics with May.

May had come to and was looking for Silas. "I'm right here," said Silas taking her hand when she murmured his name.

"How is she?" asked Silas.

"She has a concussion and needs to be taken to the hospital so they can keep an eye on her overnight," said the medic.

May shook her head and winced. "I don't want to go to the hospital. I want to go home."

"Let them take you in and check you; if there nothing else wrong, I will take you home," promised Silas.

"Okay, if you come with me," agreed May.

"I'm not letting you out of my sight," said Silas. The medics started getting May ready to go.

"Jamie, follow us to the hospital," said Silas. "I'm going to ride with May."

"Okay," agreed Jamie. He climbed into Silas' truck, and Mark led the way with his siren going.

They arrived at the hospital, and Silas followed the medics in with May. Jamie called his Dad and let him know what had happened and why they had hurried out of there the way they did.

Mark came into the waiting room where Jamie was waiting. "Silas' car is at the police station. He can pick it up there. How did he know May had been attacked?" Mark asked Jamie.

"He said May told him. All I know is, he went still as a statue, and then he was rushing out to go to May," said Jamie.

Mark smiled. "They were mind talking. Some couples, who have really strong feelings for each other, can talk to each other with their minds."

Jamie looked at Mark in disbelief and awe. "It's true," said Mark. "I have known several couples who could talk like that."

"Can you and Doris talk to each other with your minds?" asked Jamie.

"Yes, and Moon Walking can talk to any of us who will listen," said Mark.

Silas came into the waiting room. Jamie jumped up, and he and Mark turned to ask about May. "How is she?" asked Jamie.

"She is going to be alright," said Silas. "She has a concussion. They want her to stay for a couple of hours to be monitored, and then she can go home." Jamie gave a sigh of relief and Mark smiled.

"I was just telling Jamie about your car," said Mark. "It's at the police station. I will take Jamie to pick it up and bring it to the hospital. It will be much more comfortable for May going home."

"Okay," agreed Silas. "I need to get back to May. I just wanted to let you know she is alright."

As he turned to leave, his dad came into the waiting room.

"Dad," said Silas, surprised.

"How's May?" asked Adam.

"She is going to be okay. She has a bad headache, but she can go home in a couple of hours," said Silas.

Adam gave a sigh of relief and gave Silas a hug. Silas hugged him back and then left to go to May. When Silas was gone, Adam turned to Jamie and Mark.

"Did you catch the person who attacked May?" he asked Mark.

"Yes, he is in police custody. We will have to see who has jurisdiction. The attack happened on the reservation, but it was a public road. It could go either way. Judge Hawthorn will probably decide after he talks to the elders," said Mark.

"We were just about to go and pick up Silas' car and bring it to the hospital," said Jamie. "You want to come with us?"

"Yes, I will. There is nothing I can do here. I need to call your mom and let her know May is alright," said Adam.

"How did Mom find out?" asked Jamie as they started out of the hospital with Mark.

"She called me and asked me about May as I was leaving. She and May have a connection," said Adam.

As they left the hospital to go to the police station, Mark received a call on his phone. He stopped by his patrol car to talk to the caller. "I see," he said. "I'm on my way in. I'll be there shortly."

He hung up his phone and looked at Jamie and Adam.

"What has happened?" asked Jamie.

"When they took Bull in to book him, they were distracted. There was a rookie cop standing beside him, and Bull grabbed the rookie's gun. He tried to escape using the rookie as a shield. A policeman saw him backing out the door holding a gun on the rookie and told him to drop his weapon. Bull turned to fire at the policeman. Before he could fire, every policeman there opened fire on him. They aren't sure which bullets killed him, but he is dead," explained Mark.

"Wow," said Jamie. "Was the rookie hurt?"

"No, he dropped to the floor when the shooting started. He had one flesh wound, but he will be alright," answered Mark.

Mark shook his head. "Are you ready to go after Silas' car?"

"Yes, let's go," said Adam.

They all entered Mark's police car and were soon at the police station. Mark drove around to the side where Silas' car had been parked. There was a lot going on at the front. It wasn't every day there was a shooting in the front door of the police station.

Mark told them to wait while he went inside to get the keys to Silas' car. He was back quickly. He gave the keys to Jamie and, telling them he would see them later, he hurried back inside.

Jamie and Adam drove back to the hospital, and Jamie parked Silas' car beside Adam's car in the hospital parking lot. They went back inside to wait for May to be released.

They were waiting in the waiting room when Silas and May came out a couple of hours later. The nurse had insisted May had to leave in a wheelchair, so Silas was walking alongside of her chair, holding tightly to her hand while the nurse pushed the chair.

Silas asked Jamie to drive his truck home. He helped May into the front seat and fastened her seat belt. She leaned her head against the headrest and closed her eyes. Silas looked at her worriedly. He hoped she was not leaving the hospital too soon.

"Oh," said May when she thought about her purse and

the bracelet bag in the back seat. "My purse and the things I was using to work on the bracelet are in the back seat."

"Okay," said Silas with a smile. "We will get them out at home."

"Don't look in the bag. Not much is done, yet, but you are not supposed to see it," said May.

"I won't look," promised Silas. "Let's get you home and in bed."

"You know it's not going to do much good to go to bed. The doctor told you to wake me every two hours," said May.

"You'll be able to get some rest," said Silas. "You should be a lot better by morning."

"I sure am glad they gave me something for my headache," said May. "I am also glad they were able to stop the guy and get your car back."

"It's our car," said Silas. "I'm glad they caught him, too. Sometimes it pays to have a cousin who is a cop."

They pulled to a stop in front of their house. Jamie pulled up beside them and Adam parked behind him. They all got out and met beside Silas' car as he was helping May out.

"I'm glad you are alright, May," said Jamie, giving May a hug.

"Thank you, me too," said May.

Adam came forward and hugged her also and told her Myla sent her love.

"Thank her for me," said May.

"I am going to catch a ride to my place with Dad," said Jamie. "Let us know if you need us for anything."

"I will," said Silas. "Thanks for helping. I'll talk to you later. I need to get May inside so she can rest.

Jamie and Adam waved and left in Adam's car.

Silas picked May up and carried her inside. And straight on through to the bedroom where he helped her into bed.

"Don't forget to bring my stuff out of the back seat in," said May.

"I won't," promised Silas. "I'll go and get it now."

Silas brought the things in from the car and laid them on the table beside the door. He then locked the door, turned off the light, and went into the bedroom. May was still awake. She smiled at Silas as he came into the room.

Silas undressed and crawled into the bed beside May. He put his arms around her and held her close.

"I just want to hold you. I have never been so scared in my life," whispered Silas.

"I'm sorry I scared you," said May hugging Silas.

"It wasn't your fault. I am just thankful you were able to let me know so I could get to you," said Silas.

"I just called out to you in my mind and you were there," said May.

"I will always be there when you call out to me. I love you. When you call, I will answer," said Silas. "Are you hungry?"

"No, not right now, I still feel a little nauseated. Maybe later I can eat something," said May. "Are you hungry? You could go ahead and eat. You don't have to wait on me."

"I'm not hungry right now. I just want to lay here beside you and be thankful you are alright and here in my arms," said Silas.

May snuggled closer to him and savored the feel of having his arms around her. She was glad her ordeal was over and she had Silas' arms around her holding her close.

CHAPTER 10

The next morning, Silas had wanted to stay home with May, but she convinced him she was alright and he should go to work. He had awakened her through the night to check on her. May was feeling fine. Probably better than Silas. She wanted to work on her marriage bracelet. She could not work on it while Silas was home, and time was running out on her. She promised Silas she would check in with him and, if her head started bothering her again, she would call him.

After fixing breakfast for the two of them and telling Silas goodbye with a long kiss at the door, May cleaned the kitchen and then started working on her bracelet.

She had the heart finished and looked at the clock. It was nine o'clock. May smiled. "Nine o'clock and all is well," she thought.

At the lumber yard, Silas had been working on his bracelet while waiting to take a load out. When he heard May's voice in his mind, he started grinning.

"I love you," he thought.

"I love you, too," answered May.

Jamie looked over and saw Silas sitting there grinning.

"I guess May's alright," he said.

Silas looked up, startled. "How did you know I was talking to May?" he asked.

"Because you have been so solemn since you arrived here this morning. Now, I see you smiling. I know the only person who could put a smile on your face this morning is May," said Jamie.

Silas smiled. "May is fine," replied Silas. "I wasn't paying much attention when you and Mark were talking about the guy who hit May and stole the car. What are they going to do with him?"

"He's dead. He tried to escape police custody and was shot. It was Bull from the motorcycle gang. No one will have to worry about him anymore," said Jamie.

"Good," said Silas. "I was worried about May being home by herself. I am glad he is not a worry anymore. Mark and Doris are probably relieved, also."

"Yeah, I am sure they are glad to put the motorcycle gang in the past," agreed Jamie. "How are you doing on your bracelet?"

"It's coming along. Dad helped me a lot with instructions. I just want to get it finished before the wedding," said Silas.

"Just keep it simple. You will do fine," said Jamie.

"That's what Dad said," agreed Silas.

Adam came out of his office. "We have a delivery just ordered. Are you ready to go along?" he asked Silas.

"Where is it to?" asked Silas.

"It's to Rolling Fork," said Adam.

"Okay. I'll go along as long as Jamie drives. I didn't get much sleep last night. I don't think I should be driving a load," said Silas.

"No problem," said Jamie. I'll drive, and you can talk to me while you work on your bracelet."

"Good idea," agreed Silas.

Adam grinned and went back into his office.

When they were on their way, Silas decided he needed to let May know he was going to Rolling Fork.

"How's my Woodland Sprite doing?" he thought.

"I am doing fine. I was just about to take a break and fix myself a sandwich," thought May.

"I wanted to let you know that Jamie and I are delivering a load to Rolling Fork," thought Silas.

"You two be careful and don't stop at any downed tree limbs," thought May with a teasing note in her mind. Silas laughed out loud.

"What is it?" asked Jamie.

"May said for us to be careful and not to stop at any downed tree limbs," said Silas. Jamie laughed.

"I'll see you when I get back. I love you," thought Silas.

"I love you, too," responded May.

Jamie glanced over at Silas. "It is really something to know you can talk to someone with your mind," he said.

"Yeah, it is great," agreed Silas.

Jamie glanced out the window at the sky.

"Is there any chance of rain in the near future?" asked Jamie.

Silas laughed. "I don't think Moon Walking was talking about actual lightening. I think she meant your true love will appear like a bolt of lightning. You know, quick and unexpected," said Silas.

Jamie glanced at Silas and frowned. "You are not helping," he said. "I'm more confused than ever. Do I watch for lightening or not?"

Silas shrugged. "It won't hurt. Just expect the unexpected.

88

"Okay," said Jamie. "I hope it hurries up. I am so ready for something to happen."

They drove into Rolling Fork and headed for the drop-off site.

May had finished her designs on her bracelet and was working on the sides when she got a phone call from Gunner. He had made arrangements with Brenda, and they were leaving on their way to the reservation the next morning. May told them to be careful and hung up the phone.

"Hello, love," she thought.

"Are you alright?" asked Silas.

"I am fine. I just wanted to let you know Gunner and Brenda are leaving to come here in the morning," thought May.

"I'll go by and check on my house when I get back to the reservation. I want to make sure it is clean and ready for Gunner," thought Silas.

"Okay, I'll see you when you get back. Would you like me to meet you at your house?" she thought.

"No, it won't take me long and I don't think you should be driving, yet," Silas thought.

"Okay, you are probably right. I love you," thought May.

"I love you too," thought Silas.

"Is May alright?" asked Jamie.

"She is fine. She was just letting me know her brother, Gunner, and her friend, Brenda, will be starting for here in the morning," said Silas. "When we get back to the reserva-tion, could we stop by my house and check on it? I am going to loan it to Gunner while he is here and I need to be sure it is clean and has food in the refrigerator."

"Sure," agreed Jamie. "How is your bracelet coming along?"

"It's coming together," said Silas. "I am working on the sides. I have finished the design. What do you think?"

Silas held the bracelet up for Jamie to see the design.

"It looks good," said Jamie. "I hope I can do so well when my turn comes."

Silas shook his head. "You worry too much," he said.

"Yeah, I know," agreed Jamie. "I am trying to relax more. So far, it isn't working."

"Do you want to stop and get something to eat before we start home?" asked Silas.

"Sure, I could eat a hamburger. Why don't we pick some up and eat them on the way?" asked Jamie.

"Okay," agreed Silas.

They stopped at a Dairy Queen and went through the drive-through. They each ordered a burger and a milkshake. They finished them off before they reached Silas' house on the reservation. Jamie pulled to a stop on the street in front of Silas' house. Both of them climbed out and went to look over the house and see what food was there.

Silas unlocked the door and went in. The house smelled good. It had a pine smell like it had just been cleaned. They walked on through, looking around. Everything looked great. They went into the kitchen and opened the refrigerator. It was full of a variety of food. There was a piece of paper on the first shelf. It was a note from Rosa.

Silas,

Moon Walking came by and asked us to be sure your house was in good shape for May's brother. She seems determined to have him see the reservation in a good light. Myla asked me and Lone Wolf to check it out. I made a list of foods and Lone Wolf went shopping while I cleaned. I hope everything is alright. I didn't want to bother you while May was hurt, but when Moon Walking asked for something to be done, I have learned to get it done.

Love, Rosa.

Jamie had been reading over his shoulder while he read Rosa's note. "Moon Walking strikes again," he said with a laugh.

"Yeah," agreed Silas. "Well, I guess there is nothing to do here. We may as well head for the lumber yard," said Silas.

The two of them left and locked up before going on to the lumber yard.

Silas finished his beadwork on his bracelet and asked Adam about doing the straps to tie it on with. Adam showed him how they were done, and Silas did his quickly. He breathed a sigh of relief when it was finished. He hoped May's bracelet was working out okay. He put his aside and decided not to say anything about it to May just yet. He didn't want her to feel bad if she didn't finish in time for the wedding.

He was just about to head for home when May contacted him again.

"Silas, are you and Jamie ready to leave work?" asked May.

"Yes, we are just about to head out. Is something wrong?" asked Silas.

"No, I just got a call from my sister April. She is flying

into the Rolling Fork airport tonight and asked to be picked up. Are you and Jamie up for another trip to Rolling Fork today?" asked May.

"May's sister is flying into the airport in Rolling Fork tonight, and May asked if you would go with us to pick her up?" Silas asked Jamie.

"Sure," said Jamie. We can go by May's house, and all of us can go in your car," said Jamie.

"Jamie said, 'Sure.' We will be there in a little while. I love you," said Silas.

"I love you, too. Give him my thanks," said May.

"May said thanks," Silas told Jamie.

Jamie shrugged. "I am looking forward to meeting more of May's family," replied Jamie.

He and Silas told their dad good night and headed for Silas and May's home.

May was waiting for them when they arrived. They parked their trucks side by side. Jamie came in his so he would have it to go home in later. Silas would need his for work the next day. The three of them piled into the front seat of Silas' car and started for the airport.

"What time is her plane landing?" asked Silas.

"In about a half-hour," said May.

"We will be cutting it close, but we should be able to make it if the traffic is not too bad," said Jamie.

"If she had let me know sooner, I could have made arrangements to meet her. She said she was waiting on standby and didn't know until the last minute," said May.

"Don't worry, we'll get there, and if she has to wait a few minutes, she will be so glad to see you she won't care," responded Silas. May hugged his arm and smiled up at him. Silas smiled down at her and held her close. Jamie was driving.

They drove into the parking lot at the airport and, after parking, hurried inside. The plane was in the process of unloading. They stood behind the barrier and waited for the passengers to come through.

May spotted April and waved excitedly. April waved back at her and headed for May. The two girls hugged. May turned around to introduce Silas and Jamie to April. Silas gave her a hug and welcomed her. They all turned to Jamie, who was standing frozen, staring at April. April took one look at Jamie and she froze also. They stood staring at each other silently.

Jamie reached out a hand and April put her hand in his.

Silas and May gasped. "Did you see that?" asked May. "When their hands met, it looked like a spark of lightning went from one hand to the other."

"I saw it," said Silas. "Moon Walking said when Jamie met his true love, it would be like a lightning strike."

Jamie and April were still standing there, holding hands and not talking. They were just staring into each others eyes.

May nudged April. "Do you have luggage to pick up?" she asked. April nodded.

May sighed. Silas grinned. "Jamie, we have to pick up April's luggage," said Silas.

Jamie nodded. "Will you marry me?" asked Jamie. April nodded. Jamie drew her closer and kissed her.

Silas and May watched in amazement. May turned and grinned at Silas. Silas smiled back at her. "If you can get her claim check, we could go and get her luggage," said Silas.

May looked at April's purse hanging from her shoulder. She reached over and gently removed it from her shoulder and looked inside. April's claim ticket was in plain sight. She took the ticket, and she and Silas went to get the luggage. Jamie and April never knew they were gone. They were wrapped up in each other.

When May and Silas returned, May took one look at the other two still standing in the same spot kissing and shook her head

"Were we this bad?" asked May.

Silas grinned. "I know I didn't want to let go of you."

May smiled at him. "I still don't want to let go of you," she said.

Silas smiled. "Jamie, we have to go. I'll drive home. You and April can have the back seat."

Jamie pulled back from April slightly and looked at Silas and May. He looked like he was in a daze. April was still gazing at Jamie as if he was all she saw.

"I'll drive," said Silas.

"Okay," said Jamie and handed him the car keys.

They all started for the parking lot. May and Silas led and Jamie and April followed behind. He had his arm around her, and she held tightly to his hand.

Silas put the suitcases in the trunk. Jamie opened the back car door and helped April in. He climbed in after her and immediately pulled her back into his arms and started kissing her again. She made no objection.

Silas helped May into the front seat, and she scooted into the middle. He got into the driver's seat and squeezed her knee before starting the trip home.

CHAPTER 11

They arrived at May and Silas' home with little talking from the back seat. When May glanced back once, she saw April being held close in Jamie's arms with her head on his chest. They were not talking, just holding each other and being close.

They all got out of the car and started toward the porch of the house. Jamie had a firm grip on April's hand. Silas had retrieved April's luggage from the trunk and brought it in. He hesitated when he came in the door. He did not know where to take the luggage.

Jamie and April were both still in a daze. They did not look as if they were going to be far from each other any time soon.

May noticed his dilemma. "Just set her luggage inside the door of the first spare bedroom. She will decide if she is staying after she has a clearer head," said May.

Silas grinned and put the luggage inside the bedroom. He had never seen Jamie in such a daze. It was very enlightening to see his big brother acting in such a way. He wondered if he acted in the same way when he and May had gotten together.

He knew it was still hard to be away from her. He craved her presence all of the time. Just to be close to her made his heart beat faster and soothed him at the same time.

Silas thought about his Mom. She was going to be so happy to see both of her sons married happily and with families. He hoped April was as nice as May. He shook his head. Nobody could be as nice as May. April would just have to be in second place.

When he returned to the living room, May was still standing, but Jamie and April were sitting on the sofa. May turned and went into his arms and raised her face for a kiss. He obliged her. "I like being in first place," whispered May.

Silas grinned at her. It was nice to have her close enough to know what he was thinking. May just grinned and kissed him again.

May turned and looked at Jamie and April. "Jamie, you are welcome to stay here tonight if you want to," said May.

Jamie glanced at her and then at April. April was looking at him and smiling. "I just want to be where April is," he said.

"Where do you live?" asked April.

"I have a house on the reservation," said Jamie. "We can go there if you want to."

"I would love to see your house tomorrow," said April. "Right now, I just want to sit here and feel your arms around me." Jamie smiled and pulled her closer. He was all for having her in his arms.

April looked at May. "When is Gunner going to be here?" she asked.

"He is going to be here tomorrow night," said May. "He is going to be staying in Silas' house on the reservation. My friend Brenda is coming with him. She is coming for the wedding, and she and Gunner are planning on staying for a visit afterwards."

"When is the wedding?" asked April.

"It's in four days," said May. "How long is your break from school?"

"I have finished this semester. I have a two-week break. When school resumes, I won't be in regular classes. I have to decide which internship I am going o take. After a semester of internship, I will have a final test and then have to take the state test to get my license. Then I will be all set to practice."

"What are you studying?" asked Silas.

"I am in pre-law," said April.

"So you need an internship in a law office," said Silas.

"Yes," agreed April.

"Our Uncle, Glen Black Feather, has a law office on the reservation. I know he has been very busy, and one of the ladies he had working in his office has left. He may be able to offer you an internship," said Silas.

Jamie started smiling. He looked at April. "You would be able to stay here and marry me," he said.

"Yes," agreed April. "I would have to talk to Mr. Black Feather first. It would be great to work in his office. He is a great lawyer. I have attended a couple of lectures he gave at the university. He is very awe-inspiring."

"I think you would like him and his family," said May. "The ladies in the family are very nice. One of his daughters-in-law came by to visit. She has a beautiful new baby. She's a sweetheart."

"You always were a soft touch for a new baby," said April smiling.

"Yeah, I guess so," agreed May smiling at Silas. He smiled back at her. He remembered seeing May holding the baby. She had looked so natural. He was looking forward to seeing a baby of their own in her arms. May smiled at him. She had picked up on his thoughts. She was looking forward to holding a child of theirs also.

"Are any of you hungry? I can fix us something to eat," said May.

"I ate on the plane," said April.

"We had a hamburger and shake before we came home," said Silas.

"Well, if anyone gets hungry, just help yourselves. There are plenty of sandwich makings in the refrigerator," said May. "What about something to drink?"

Everyone was shaking their heads.

Jamie looked at April. "I was serious about marrying you. Did you mean it when you said yes?"

"Yes," April was nodding her head. "Anytime, anywhere."

Jamie grinned. "Well, how about in four days. We could have a double wedding with May and Silas. All the arrangements have been made. All we would need is a marriage license." Jamie looked at May and Silas. "You wouldn't mind, would you?"

May and Silas were smiling. "I think it would be great," said May. "If that is what April wants. Are you sure you would not like your own separate ceremony?"

"I would love to have a double wedding with you. I think it would make it more special," said April.

"It settled then," said Silas. "We can call Derrick Bear in the morning and have him prepare another license for the two of you, and we will be all set."

Jamie and April smiled at each other and then at May and Silas. "Should we call Mom and Dad and let them know?" asked April.

"You can if you want to," said May. Serin is bringing Autumn and the boys, and Gunner and Brenda are coming. I didn't call Mom because I wanted a peaceful wedding, but you can call her if you want to."

"I will call Dad. I'll tell him if she causes trouble, I'll have her detained," said April laughing. May laughed also.

"Are you two going to live in your house on the reservation after you are married?" asked Silas.

"If it's alright with April," said Jamie. He looked at April. "I have a three-bedroom house on the reservation. If you don't like it, we will look for something else. We could even build us a new place if you want to."

April smiled at Jamie and placed her hands on his face. "It will be fine. It doesn't matter where we live as long as we are together." Jamie leaned forward and kissed her.

May smiled at them and then looked at Silas. He was also smiling. She knew she felt the same way about Silas, and he was in agreement completely.

May grimaced slightly. Silas looked at her closely.

"Is your head hurting?" asked Silas worriedly.

"Just a little," said May.

"Do you want something for it? Do you want to lie down?" asked Silas.

"No, it's not that bad. I'll take something, but I'm not ready to lie down yet," said May.

"Okay, I'll get you some water and medicine," said Silas.

He went to get water and medicine. April looked at May. Silas' worry had caught her attention.

"Is something wrong?" she asked. "Are you sick?"

"No, I'm fine. It's just a headache," said May.

"It's probably from the bump on your head," said Jamie.

"What bump on the head?" asked April.

"May was carjacked. She was hit on the head. She was checked out at the hospital, but she will probably have headaches for a few days," said Silas coming back into the room with May's water and medicine. He handed them to May, and she took the medicine and washed it down with the water.

"What? You were carjacked!" exclaimed April.

"Yes, it was partly my fault. There was a downed tree limb in the road, and I got out to move it and I was knocked out and my car was taken," said May.

"Oh, my God. Are you sure you are alright?" asked April.

"How did you get help?" asked April.

"I was able to mind talk to Silas, and he came and called for help," said May.

"What's mind talk?" asked April.

"It's where I think something and send it to Silas, and he hears me and answers," said May.

April looked at May and Silas, then she looked at Jamie. "Will we be able to do that?" she asked.

"I don't know. We just have to wait and see," said Jamie.

"It sounds cool. I think I would like to be able to talk to you without anyone else hearing," said April smiling.

"Yeah, me too," agreed Jamie.

April looked back at May. "Are you sure you're okay? If you need to lie down, don't mind us. We can take care of ourselves."

"I'll see. Give the medicine time to work," said May.

"Did they catch the carjacker?" asked April.

"Yes, when I heard what happened, I had Jamie call our cousin Mark Black Feather. He's on the police force in Rolling Fork. He had a roadblock set up and they caught the guy," said Silas.

"Good," said April. "What happens next?"

"It's over. He was shot trying to escape police custody," said Jamie.

"What? You didn't tell me he was shot," said May.

"I just found out today. After you told me April was coming, I forgot about it," said Silas.

May squeezed his hand to let him know everything was alright. "How bad was he hurt?" asked May.

"He didn't make it," said Silas.

"Oh," said May. She tried to think about how she felt about that. All she really felt was a sense of relief.

"I think I will lie down, if you don't mind," said May.

"I don't mind at all," said April. "You get some rest. I'll see you in the morning."

May stopped by the sofa, and April rose to give her a hug. "Your luggage is in the first bedroom. The bathroom is down the hall. If you need anything just help yourself," said May.

"I will be fine. Jamie will look after me. Go and rest," said April.

"Alright, goodnight, I am glad you are here. Goodnight, Jamie," said May.

"Goodnight, May, I hope your head feels better," said Jamie rising and giving her a hug.

"Thank you, I'll be fine."

"Goodnight," said Silas, hugging April and Jamie and following May into the bedroom.

"Are you sure you are alright?" asked Silas.

"I am fine. It's just a little headache. I just wanted to give April and Jamie some time alone to get to know each other, and I wanted to feel your arms around me," said May, turning and going into his arms.

Silas' arms closed around her, and he drew her close and kissed her.

Silas pulled back reluctantly after the kiss.

"Do you need any help getting ready for bed?" he asked.

May smiled. "I would love some help getting out of these clothes. Can I help you get out of your clothes?"

"I think I can manage," said Silas with a grin.

"Party pooper," said May with a mock frown.

Silas grinned. "You can help next time when you don't have a headache," he promised as he pulled a gown from the drawer and helped May into it. He took her other clothes and dropped them in the clothes hamper. He helped May into bed and crawled in beside her and drew her into his arms.

May snuggled close to Silas and enjoyed the feel of him close.

"I love you," she said.

"I love you, too," said Silas as he kissed her.

With a sigh of satisfaction, they settled into each other's arms and closed their eyes for sleep.

Jamie leaned back into the armrest on the end of the sofa. April stretched out beside him and laid her face on his chest. His arms were holding her close. They lay there quietly, talking and kissing often. They talked about their lives, their goals and where they hoped to go from the point they were at. They both got drowsier and drowsier. Finally, sleep overtook them and they both fell asleep there in each other's arms.

When May and Silas emerged from their room the next morning, they were surprised to find April and Jamie sound asleep on the sofa in each other's arms. They went quietly into the kitchen, and while May prepared breakfast, Silas filled the coffee maker and put cups out for coffee. He also set the sugar bowl and creamer on the table.

May made scrambled eggs and bacon. She put rolls in the oven to brown and set out the butter and jelly.

They were putting food on the table when April and Jamie came into the room.

"I smell coffee," said April.

"Coffee always did wake you up," said May with a smile.

"Yeah, I need my coffee to get me going in the morning," agreed April.

"Breakfast is ready. Have a seat," said May, motioning for them to sit at the table.

Silas poured everyone coffee and placed it on the table. April took a big drink of hers and sighed happily.

Everyone laughed at her enjoyment of her coffee.

"Good morning, Jamie. I hope you like your eggs scrambled," said May.

"Good morning," said Jamie. "I love my eggs scrambled. Thanks." May and Silas joined them at the table and they all dug in.

"Do you guys have to work today?" asked May.

"We will have to go by and check in with Dad, but we can take the day off. We have a lot to do to get ready for the wedding. We also have to call Derrick about the license. We need to take April by to see Uncle Glen, and we need to go see Mom," said Silas.

"We can take my truck in, and April can take her luggage to my house. She can stay with me," said Jamie.

"We have to be sure and be back here before Gunner and Brenda arrive," said May. "Since you are not going to work, we can take the car and leave your truck here," May told Silas.

"Yeah, I'll feel better if you are not driving yet," said Silas.

"How's your head this morning?' asked April.

"It is fine," said May. "Let's just pile the dishes in the dishwasher, and we can get started."

They made quick work of clearing the table and were soon on their way.

Jamie led the way, and Silas followed. They were soon on the reservation. When they started past the community center, they spotted Moon Walking waiting for them. Jamie pulled to a stop and Silas stopped behind him. They all got out to speak with Moon Walking.

"Hello, Moon Walking," greeted Jamie and Silas

"This is April. She is May's sister," said Silas.

"Yes, your Shrinking Violet has produced beautiful daughters. Welcome home, April Showers," said Moon Walking.

"I notified Little Bear to bring another marriage license with him to the wedding. I warned him the lightning had struck," said Moon Walking.

"You will do very well with Glen Black Feather. He will be good training for you, and he is a fair man," Moon Walking assured April.

"Thank you," said April faintly.

"Good morning, May Flower. I am glad you did not suffer any lasting effects from your run-in with Bull," said Moon Walking.

"Good morning, Moon Walking. I'm fine, thank you. Thank you for helping us with the wedding," said May.

Moon Walking nodded her head graciously. "I will let you young people go and spread your good news." Moon Walking turned and walked back into the community center.

April was standing with an astonished look on her face. "Is she for real? How did she know all about us? We hadn't told anyone," said April.

"Moon Walking knows everything and she helps everyone on the reservation. It is a privilege to be on her radar," said May.

"What did she mean about Shrinking Violet having beautiful daughters?" asked April.

"Shrinking Violet was Mother's Indian name. Dancing Eagle told me years ago. I never told anyone about it," said May. "Dancing Eagle said when Mother was born, the fields were full of violets, but every time anyone tried to hold Mother, she would shrink away from them and cry."

April nodded. "I hope everyone is not going to start calling me April Showers," said April.

May laughed. "They are already beginning to call me May Flower," said May.

April looked at Jamie. He looked like he was about to say something. "Don't even think about it," she warned.

They all laughed and piled back into their vehicles to go on to the lumber yard.

CHAPTER 12

$\mathcal{G}$unner stopped at Brenda's apartment to pick her up. He had called her the night before to remind her they would be leaving early. He just hoped she was ready. He knocked on her door and waited. There was no answer. He knocked again. He heard someone mumble something inside.

When the door opened, he was surprised to see Brenda dressed and ready to go. "I was just finishing my packing," said Brenda with a smile.

She stood back to let Gunner enter. He entered the apartment and looked around. It was neat but compact.

"Where's your luggage? I'll take it to the car," offered Gunner.

Brenda led the way to her bedroom and pointed at the pile of luggage.

Gunner looked at the pile and grinned. He picked up three cases. One was in each hand and one was under his arm.

"Can you get the door? I'll be right back for the rest," said Gunner.

"Sorry there's so many, but we are staying a couple of

months, and I had to have something special for the wedding," said Brenda.

"Not a problem," said Gunner as he went out the door Brenda held open for him. He went to his car and set the cases down while he opened the trunk and shifted his two cases around and loaded Brenda's in. There was room for a couple of more cases. The rest would have to go into the back seat.

Gunner started back and met Brenda coming with two more cases. He took them from her and put them in the trunk. When he closed the trunk, Brenda looked at him. He smiled.

"The rest will go in the back seat," he said.

"Okay," agreed Brenda.

They went back inside, and Gunner took the rest of the luggage to the car while Brenda went around and checked the stove and made sure the apartment was locked. Gunner started back, but when he saw Brenda locking the door, he waited by the car and opened her door for her to get in. He then went around and got in the driver's seat. He looked at Brenda and smiled.

"Already to go," he said.

Brenda smiled back at him. "Yes, let's get the show on the road," she replied.

Gunner laughed softly. This was going to be the start of a great adventure. He was finally going to be able to get to know Brenda and see if this attraction he had for her was the lasting kind and if she felt the same. He wasn't sure if Brenda was really attracted to him or if she just liked to flirt.

Brenda heard his laugh and smiled to herself. She was going on a trip with Gunner Merril. She had time to see if he could ever feel anything for her. She was looking forward to the challenge of the time with him. She planned to take advantage of every opportunity. She was super excited.

Brenda looked over at Gunner. Her dream and he was sitting right beside her. She pinched her arm.

"Ouch," said Brenda. Gunner looked at her. "Sorry," said Brenda. "I just wanted to be sure I wasn't dreaming."

Gunner laughed. "It's no dream. We are headed for May's wedding and are going to be spending a lot of time together," he said with satisfaction.

"Good," said Brenda. "I was beginning to think I would have to kidnap you to spend any time with you."

"No kidnapping required," said Gunner. "We have a chance to learn more about each other."

"What do you want to know?" asked Brenda.

"Do you like your job?" asked Gunner.

"Not really; it's okay but it's mostly filing work. It's very boring, but it pays the bills," said Brenda.

"So you wouldn't mind doing something else?" asked Gunner.

Brenda looked at him curiously. "Why, do you know of a job for me?"

"No, I was just wondering if you would be willing to move," said Gunner.

"Sure, if a good opportunity presented itself," replied Brenda. "May is my best friend, and she is not going to be there anymore."

"Yeah, I am going to miss her," agreed Gunner. "The phone is not the same as knowing she is there, and I can pop in and see her."

"Yeah," agreed Brenda. "It's not the same at all."

"Do you have any family?" asked Gunner.

"I have my mom and dad. Dad retired a few years ago and they sold out and moved to Florida. I was a little surprise for them when they had given up trying to have a family. They didn't seem to know what to do with me. They were overwhelmed. Don't get me wrong. I love them, and they love me. It's just they were a couple for so long they were ready to go back to being a couple again," explained Brenda.

"I still think they should have thought twice about moving off and leaving you by yourself," said Gunner.

Brenda smiled and patted his arm. "I'm fine. I keep in touch with them, and if I needed anything, they would be there for me. I could have gone with them, but I didn't want to."

Gunner shook his head. "I am glad you are alright, but when I have a family, I am not going to let them feel alone. I will probably smother them with attention," he said with a laugh.

Brenda smiled. "I think you will make a great dad," said Brenda.

Gunner looked at her and smiled. "You do?"

"Yes," nodded Brenda.

Gunner looked back at the road. He smiled with satisfaction.

After they had driven for a couple of hours, Gunner glanced at Brenda. She had been sitting quietly for a while. "Would you like to stop for breakfast? We are coming up on a small town," said Gunner.

"Sure," agreed Brenda "I would love some coffee. It would be nice to stretch my legs a bit."

"Okay, we will stop at IHOP. We can fill up on gas afterward," said Gunner.

They enjoyed their breakfast. They didn't hurry, but they didn't waste time either. They still had a long trip ahead of them. When they were finished and leaving, Gunner took Brenda's arm to guide her to the car. When they were beside the car, Brenda started to turn to get in the car. Gunner stopped her and turned her to face him.

"I was wondering about something," he said, gazing into her eyes with a grin on his face.

Brenda smiled up at him. "What's that?" she asked.

"I was wondering if your lips were as kissable as they looked," said Gunner.

Brenda smiled. "There's only one way to find out," she replied. Brenda raised her lips and touched his. Gunner took charge and deepened the kiss. When he drew back, they were both breathless.

"Wow," said Brenda.

Gunner grinned. "Yeah, definitely kissable," he said.

He opened the car door and waited for Brenda to get in before shutting it. He drove to the nearest gas station and filled up with gas. When they were back on the road, Brenda looked at Gunner.

"Why did you decide to kiss me now?" she asked.

"I am thinking about making some major changes in my life. I have been thinking about you for awhile, and I wanted to know how you felt about me before I made any major decisions," said Gunner.

"You have been thinking about me?" asked Brenda.

"Yes, I have," said Gunner.

"I have been thinking about you, too," said Brenda.

"I wasn't sure if you really meant it or if you were just flirting," said Gunner.

"I meant it. I was too uncertain about your feelings to come right and tell you. Flirting is my defense mechanism," admitted Brenda. "I have been having feelings for you for a while."

"I am attracted to you also," admitted Gunner.

Brenda was silent for a minute, thinking. "What changes?" she asked.

Gunner looked at her and then back at the road.

"I was thinking about moving to Rolling Fork if I can hook up with a good job," said Gunner.

"Does May know?" asked Brenda.

"No, I haven't told anyone but you. I wanted to see how you would feel about moving to Rolling Fork if we get together," said Gunner.

"I want to look around before I make up my mind," said Brenda after thinking about it.

"Fair enough," said Gunner.

"If you want to move there, that would be a major plus for me. I want to explore our feelings for each other," said Brenda.

Gunner grinned at her. "So do I," he said. "So do I."

Brenda smiled and laid her head back. She had a lot to think about. "Gunner kissed me," she thought.

"Yes, I did," thought Gunner.

Brenda sat up straight.

"You heard me. I heard you," she said.

"Yes, I did. Yes, you did," agreed Gunner with a grin.

"How did we do it?" asked Brenda.

"It means we are meant for each other. In the Indian community, true mates can mind talk to each other," said Gunner.

"Wow," said Brenda. "I wonder if May and Silas can mind talk."

"I wouldn't be surprised if they could. If they have tried," said Gunner.

"We really are meant to be together," said Brenda.

"Yes, we are. Our feelings will only grow stronger as time passes," said Gunner.

Brenda undid her seat belt and moved into the middle and fastened the belt there. She wanted to be closer to Gunner. Gunner laid a hand on her knee and squeezed gently. Brenda laid her head on his shoulder and smelled his unique scent. It was all Gunner's. She loved his smell. She had been getting close to him for years just so she could breathe in his fragrance.

While Brenda and Gunner continued their trip, May and April went by and talked to Glen Black Feather. He remembered meeting April when he lectured at the university. He offered her an internship in his office, and she accepted. He was very happy she was marrying Jamie.

"I am going to have two new nieces in my family at once," said Glen. "Welcome to our family, both of you." He gave both of them a hug and shook Silas and Jamie's hands.

After leaving the law office, April called their dad and invited him and their mother to the wedding. He said he would let her know if they could make it. It was awful short notice. She told him Serin and the boys would be coming with Autumn. He still had to talk to their mother and call them back.

"Let's go out and see Myla," suggested May. She turned to April. "You are going to love Jamie and Silas' mom. She is so sweet."

May and Silas went in the car, and Jamie and April went in his truck. Rosa met them at the door and welcomed them. She gave May and Silas a hug and then turned to April and Jamie.

"You did good, Jamie," she said, giving them both a hug. "Your mom is out in the gazebo. Go on out the back. Your dad called and gave her the news. She is very pleased."

They all went through to the back and out to the garden and gazebo. Myla was sitting in the same place as she was the last time May had visited her.

"Hello, Myla," said May as they approached her. She did not want Myla to be startled.

Myla looked up and smiled. She rose from her seat as they

approached. She waited until they reached her before she spoke.

"Hello, May. This must be your sister," she said, looking at April.

"Yes, this is April. April, this is Jamie's mom, Myla."

"It's nice to meet you," said April.

"I am glad you and Jamie found each other," said Myla.

"So am I," agreed April with a smile.

Jamie and Silas both came forward and kissed Myla on her cheek. "You don't mind us having a double wedding with May and Silas do you?" asked Jamie.

"I can't think of anything more perfect," said Myla. "You and Silas have been so close all of your lives. It stands to reason you would marry on the same day." Myla smiled. "And to marry sisters," she added.

Jamie and Silas both hugged their ladies and smiled lovingly at them.

"We just wanted to come by and see you, but we have a lot to get done in the next three days. So, we will see you later," said Jamie. "I still have to show April my house."

"All right, thanks for coming by. Remember, girls, you are welcome here anytime, and if you need any help just call. I'll send Rosa right over," said Myla with a laugh.

They all laughed with her, but Silas and Jamie looked stunned. When they got outside at the car and truck, Jamie and Silas looked at each other. "Mom made a joke," said Jamie. Silas nodded.

"What's wrong with that?" asked April. "Everyone makes jokes."

"Mom doesn't," said Jamie. "At least, she didn't before."

They all piled into their vehicles and headed for Jamie's house. When they pulled to a stop in front of Jamie's house, they stood looking around for a minute.

"It looks nice, Jamie," said May.

"Yes, it does," agreed April.

Jamie flushed slightly. He had been worried about April liking his place. "Let's go inside," said Jamie.

Silas grinned at Jamie as they went inside. He knew Jamie had been worried.

When Jamie opened the door and stood back for them to enter, April squeezed his hand before going inside. Jamie squeezed her hand also.

When they got inside, the girls started wandering around looking at everything. The guys followed along, listening to the girls talk. Jamie finally relaxed when he understood they really liked his place.

May went over and stood close to Silas. He put his arm around her. "Is there a place close to Rolling Fork where we can rent cabins for a few days? I need to see about getting a place for Serin and Autumn and the boys and one for Mom and Dad," asked May.

"I don't know. We could ask Dad. He might know," said Silas.

"I don't want to ask any of your relatives. They would offer to take them in, and I don't want to put anyone out. Besides, Mom can be hard to take," said May.

"I wouldn't mind Serin, Autumn, and the boys staying with us, but we won't have room. Brenda is going to be staying with us," said May.

April looked at Jamie. He smiled and nodded his head. "Your Mom and Dad can stay with us," said Jamie. "We have three bedrooms." He looked at May and Silas. "You can bunk the boys down in sleeping bags in your living room. Tell them they are camping out. They will love it," said Jamie.

May smiled and hugged Silas. "What a great idea," said May.

"If you want it to be authentic, we can put up a big tent and have a real camp out," said Silas. "We can camp at least for one night if it doesn't rain."

"The boys will love it," said May. "Do you have a tent?"

"Yes, Jamie and I used to have camp outs all of the time," said Silas.

"Okay, let's go home and wait for Brenda and Gunner," said May. "We need to let April and Jamie get settled in."

"We'll see you guys later," said Silas as he and May headed for home.

May settled back in the seat beside Silas.

"This wedding is beginning to draw a crowd," said May. Silas just smiled at her. "Are we going anywhere after the wedding?" asked May.

"You mean a honeymoon," said Silas.

"Yes," agreed May.

"Do you want to go away?" asked Silas.

"No," said May. "I just to run everyone off, barricade the door, and have you all to myself for a week or two."

"We will have to see what can be arranged," said Silas. "I like your idea. Maybe we can work something out."

CHAPTER 13

*G*unner and Brenda were enjoying their trip. They spent their time talking and learning about each other. They sat close to each other. It seemed as if they had to be touching. When they stopped and filled up with gas, it was only about another three hours drive to May and Silas' house. They decided to get something to eat. They sat next to each other in the booth and enjoyed the closeness.

"Silas is lending me his house to stay in while I am there," said Gunner. "Would you stay with me?"

Brenda looked into his eyes and grinned. "Yes," she said.

Gunner smiled and leaned over and kissed her.

When the kiss ended, Brenda glanced at the counter and saw the checkers watching them. "I'm not complaining, but as much as I love your kisses, I think we are drawing a lot of attention," said Brenda.

Gunner looked around and smiled. Everyone suddenly found something else to look at. "They are just jealous because they don't have someone as gorgeous as you to kiss," said Gunner.

Brenda laughed. "I love you, too," she said. "Did anyone ever tell you that you have an intimidating look, sometimes?"

"It has been mentioned on occasion," admitted Gunner.

"You have never been intimidated. It was the first thing I noticed about you. After your gorgeous body, of course," said Gunner.

"Well," said Brenda. "The first thing I noticed about you was your smell."

"My smell!" exclaimed Gunner. "Are you telling me I stink?"

"No, you smell great. I used to get as close to you as I could just so I could breathe you in," admitted Brenda with a smile.

"Well, I'll be," said Gunner with a smile. "I guess I need to write my deodorant company a thank you letter."

Brenda laughed. "Your scent is uniquely Gunner. Even if someone else used the same deodorant, they would not have the same scent."

"Thanks, I think," said Gunner with a smile. "We had better get going. May will be expecting us."

"Okay," said Brenda. They threw away their trash and resumed their journey.

May and Silas were at home enjoying time alone. So much had been going on, they had not been able to relax and enjoy each other's company. They had not been there long when the phone rang.

May sat up on the sofa, where she had been enjoying Silas' kisses, and answered the phone. It was Serin letting her know they would be there the next day. She assured him they were prepared for them and saying goodbye, hung up her phone. The phone started ringing again. This time it was Rosa's granddaughter, Shala.

"Hi, Shala," said May. "Your grandmother told us you were looking for work."

"Yes, Ma'am, I am. Grandmom said I would not be able to live in at first, until after the wedding," said Shala.

"No, we will have a house full for a few days. I would love to have you come in for the next few days, but I will not need anyone for two weeks after the wedding. If that will work for you, I can offer you a live-in position then," said May.

"You want me to come by in the morning? We can meet, and I can straighten the house and maybe cook a meal," said Shala.

"Okay. What time do you want to come by?" asked May.

"Is nine o'clock okay?" asked Shala.

"Nine o'clock will be fine. I'll see you then," said May.

Silas smiled and pulled May back into his arms after she hung up the phone.

After a couple of kisses, May leaned back and looked at him. "Do you know what shape the apartment over the garage is in?" she asked.

"No," said Silas. "There has been so much going on, I haven't had a chance to explore it," said Silas.

"I was thinking. If we could fix it up, Shala could live there. She would have her own place, and we would have more privacy," said May.

"Good idea, we will have to check it out when we can spare a minute or two," laughed Silas.

May laughed also. "I know what you mean. It was just a thought."

"It was a good thought. We will have more time to explore it after we are married and send everyone home," said Silas.

May looked at Silas and put her hands on his face. "I love you," she whispered.

"My woodland sprite, I adore you," said Silas, kissing her passionately.

They lay on the sofa, enjoying each other until they heard a car stop outside. May groaned as they got up to see if Gunner and Brenda had arrived, Silas opened the door and they went out onto the porch. It was indeed Gunner and Brenda.

Brenda and Gunner came forward to greet them. Gunner had a firm hold on Brenda's hand. He had to turn her loose to hug May and shake hands with Silas. Brenda hugged May and then Silas.

"I love your house," said Brenda, looking around. "It looks very nice," agreed Gunner.

"Are you going to bring Brenda's luggage in so we can take you to Silas' house?" asked May.

Gunner put his arm around Brenda and hugged her close. "Brenda is going to be staying with me," he said, smiling at her. Brenda smiled back at him and nodded at May, who was looking at her inquiringly.

"Okay, I know you two are tired, so we need to show you the way to Silas' house so you can rest," said May.

Silas got May's purse and locked the house while May talked with Brenda. Then Brenda and Gunner got into his car and May and Silas climbed into their car. Gunner turned his car and followed Silas out to the road and onto the road leading to the reservation.

When they pulled to a stop in front of Silas' house, they all piled out and stood looking at the house while Silas went and unlocked the door.

"How did a bachelor keep a house looking and smelling so nice?" asked Brenda.

"She has a thing about smell," laughed Gunner. Brenda punched him lightly on the arm and smiled at him.

"Mom's housekeeper gave it the once over," said Silas.

"She also stocked the refrigerator. So help yourselves to whatever is there," said Silas.

"I'll help you bring in your luggage, then we will get out of your way and let you rest," said Silas.

Gunner and Silas went out to get their luggage, and May turned to Brenda and smiled. "So, you and Gunner," she said.

"Yes," agreed Brenda, "I have had feelings for him for a while, but I didn't think I had a chance with him. You don't mind, do you?"

"How could I mind?" said May. She gave Brenda a hug, "My best friend and my brother. I couldn't think of anything better except maybe the two of you moving here so we can see each other."

"Maybe, who knows," shrugged Brenda.

Silas came over and put his arm around May. "We are done. Are you ready to go?" he asked.

"Yes," agreed May. "We'll see you tomorrow," she gave Gunner and Brenda a hug and she and Silas left.

Brenda turned to Gunner and smiled. Gunner opened his arms and Brenda walked into them. They closed around her tightly, and he proceeded to kiss her passionately.

"Well," said May as they were driving home. "I guess we won't need the tent. We have plenty of room for Autumn, Serin, and the boys."

"The tent would have been fun," said Silas. "Maybe we could have the boys for a visit in the summer and have a camp out then."

"I'll suggest it to Serin and see what I can arrange," promised May.

"When Autumn finds out about you setting up trust funds for the boys, she may be easier to persuade to let them come for a visit," said Silas.

"Maybe, I'm not going to get into it at our wedding. I don't want any conflict. This is about us. I want happy memories," said May.

Silas reached over and clasped her hand. He had to turn it loose to turn into the drive to their house, but as soon as he parked, he pulled her into his arms and kissed her.

When they came up for air, May smiled at Silas. "Not that I am complaining, but why don't we go inside?"

Silas laughed. "I couldn't wait," he said.

"Whenever you get to where you can wait," said May earnestly, "I will know something is wrong."

They climbed out of the car and headed for the door with Silas' arm around May's shoulder, holding her close to his side. May smiled up at him with love in her eyes.

"My beautiful woodland sprite," said Silas lovingly.

When they went inside, May led the way to the kitchen and looked in the refrigerator to see what she could fix for them to eat.

"Would you like an omelet?" she asked.

"Sure, are you up to making it? How is your head?" asked Silas.

"My head is fine. It won't take long to make an omelet," said May, getting things out of the refrigerator and placing them on the counter. She took down a bowl and a fork and placed them on the counter. Next, she got a pan out and put it on the stove to warm and melt some butter. Silas watched her with a smile. She looked so efficient.

"Put some plates and forks on the table and pour us some iced tea," said May.

"Yes, Ma'am," said Silas with a salute.

May turned and looked at him.

"I'm sorry. I didn't mean to be bossy," said May.

Silas laughed. "I love your bossy side. I don't mind helping. We get done faster and can get down to the fun part of the evening."

May smiled. "I'm all for the fun part of the evening," she said.

While she had been talking, she had mixed the ingredients and, after seasoning them, poured them into the pan to cook. She watched them closely and turned them at just the right time. After cutting the omelet in half, she placed it on two plates.

Silas had made some toast and put two slices on each plate. The two of them sat down to a quickly made, but good tasting, meal.

After cleaning the kitchen, locking up, and taking a shower together, the two of them settled into bed in each other's arms.

May sighed. This was a closeness she hoped never to lose.

"You won't lose it," said Silas. "I will always hold you close."

May snuggled closer to Silas and kissed him.

May received a text from Serin the next morning. May's parents were following Serin and Autumn on the trip. They were coming to the wedding. He wanted May to be aware they were coming. May thanked him for the text and let him know she knew they were coming.

Shala arrived at nine. May and Silas welcomed her. Silas and Jamie had known her for years. She had visited often with Rosa.

May invited her in and showed her around. There was not much for her to do at the present time. Silas and May had been cleaning up after themselves. May explained about her sister and her boys being there for the wedding.

"I don't know how long they are planning to stay," said May. "I'll have to find out when they get here."

"Do you have a large family, Shala?" asked May.

"Yes, I have three sisters and two brothers. We live in a three-bedroom house," said Shala. "You can understand why I am looking for a live-in job.

"I certainly can. It can seem like you never get a moment to yourself. There is always someone there," said May.

"Yes," agreed Shala.

Silas had been outside while May had been showing Shala around and talking to her. He came back inside. "Ladies, I have something to show you," said Silas. He motioned for them to follow him.

He led them around a small orchard to a garage. He opened the door and led them inside. He turned the light on and led the way around some boxes. Some old furniture was stored there also.

"I hadn't thought about this place until May mentioned it. I decided to go exploring," said Silas. He led the way up some stairs and opened a door at the top. He reached in and turned on a light.

May walked in and looked around. "It looks like Moon Walking had this place taken care of, also," said May.

It had a small sitting room. There was a combination dining and kitchen area. They found a bedroom and bathroom.

"What do you think?" May asked Shala.

"It's very nice," said Shala.

"Do you think you would like living here?" asked May.

"You want me to live here?" asked Shala. She looked around in amazement.

"Only if you think you will like it," said May.

"I would love it," said Shala. She looked as if she was about to cry.

Silas had been standing back, letting them talk and work things out. "You don't think you would be afraid out here away from the house?" asked Silas.

Shala started shaking her head. "It's not far from the house. Look on the wall. There is a calling device. If I need help, I can use it or my phone. I would love having my own place. My dad can not complain, because I will be working for you and May, and he would not want to do anything to upset your mom. It is great," said Shala.

"It is settled," said May. "You can move in anytime you want to. You don't have to wait until after the wedding."

"Is your family coming to the wedding?" asked Silas.

"Of course," said Shala. "They are very excited to see both you and Jamie getting married."

They went back to the house, and May found a key for the garage apartment hanging by the back door. She gave the key to Shala and told her to go and get her things so she could move in.

"You can eat here until you can buy some food," said May.

"Okay, I'll see you in awhile," said a very happy Shala.

May and Silas smiled as they watched a smiling Shala leave to get her things.

CHAPTER 14

*M*ay and Silas went back to the house. They had barely gotten inside before they heard a car outside.

"It's too soon for my family," said May.

Silas opened the door and went out onto the porch. May followed him out. When Silas saw who was there, he started grinning.

"Hello, Marcel," he said to the person standing by his truck. "Hello, Stanley," he said to the person on the other side of the truck. Marcel and Stanley returned his greeting and started for the porch.

"May, this is Marcel Black Feather and Stanley White. Gentlemen, this is the love of my life, soon to be wife, May Merril," said Silas.

"Howdy, Ma'am," said Stanley.

"Hello, May," said Marcel. "Welcome to our family."

"Hello," said May. "Come on inside. I am glad you stopped by." May turned and led the way inside.

"Dad told me you might be interested in letting us lease

some of your land for our horses," said Marcel after taking a seat.

"Would either of you like something to drink? I have iced tea or a soda," asked May.

"No, thank you, we are fine," said Marcel.

"I told your dad I might be interested in leasing some of my land. The land I am talking about joins the land being leased by the mine. Would that be a problem?" asked May.

"No," said Marcel. "We are already using our land joining the mine for raising the horses. The mine doesn't bother the horses."

"There is a small house on the property. I don't know what shape it is in. I haven't had time to check it out, but it might be alright for someone to live in and look after the horses," said May.

"Why don't you and Logan look over the land and house and see if it will suit you?" said Silas. "You can get back in touch with us in a couple of weeks. We are not going to do anything with it before the wedding."

Marcel smiled at him. "Okay, congratulations to you and your lovely bride. Is there any more lovely ladies where you came from?" asked Marcel.

"Not anymore," said May with a smile. "My sister April is marrying Jamie and my friend Brenda is with my brother, Gunner. You are out of luck."

Silas and Stanley both laughed at Marcel's look. Marcel sighed. "Always too slow," he said, getting up to go.

Silas tapped him on his shoulder. "Patience, cousin, there's hope for you, yet."

"It is easy for you to say," said Marcel. "You have already found your love. Do you know how lucky you are?"

Silas put his arm around May and held her close. "Yes, I do," he said. May squeezed him back and smiled.

"We'll look around and get back in touch with you in a couple of weeks," said Marcel. "It was nice to meet you, May."

"Ma'am," said Stanley nodding his head as he followed Marcel out.

"Doris told me to see if your nephews are going to be here tomorrow," said Marcel when they were on the porch.

"Yes, they are going to be here tonight," said May. "Why?"

"She's having a birthday party for her brother, Orin, tomorrow. It starts at eleven in the morning. There will be pony rides for the youngsters. They will have games and lots of food, including cake and ice cream. She told me to tell you the boys would be welcome. It will be at her and Mark's house," said Marcel.

"I'll tell them about it when they get here. I'm sure they would love the pony rides and having other youngsters to play with," said May. "Tell Doris I will let her know and thank her for the invitation."

"Sure, we'll be in touch about the land," said Marcel.

May and Silas stood on the porch and watched as Marcel turned his truck and left. They were turning to go inside when Shala drove by them and around to the back where the garage was.

"I'll go help her take her things upstairs," said Silas. He gave May a quick kiss and started for the garage apartment. May turned and went inside.

May called April to let her know their parents were on their way, following Autumn and Serin.

"If you could be over here about six, you could show them the way to your place," said May.

"Okay," said April. "I'll get Jamie to drive me over. Let me know if any plans change."

"Okay," agreed May.

May went into their bedroom and took out the marriage

bracelet. She checked it over to be sure it was ready. It looked fine to her. She carefully wrapped it in a cloth and put it away. "I wonder if Silas finished his bracelet," said May.

"Yes, I did," thought Silas.

May laughed. "I finished mine, too," she thought.

"I'm glad," thought Silas. "I will look forward to wearing it. I love you."

"I love you, too," thought May.

May smiled as she went to check the refrigerator to make sure they had plenty of child-friendly food. It looked good to her. They would be at the birthday party tomorrow and the wedding was the next day. The boys should not be too bored.

Silas came in the back door.

"Is Shala all settled in?" asked May.

"I carried her things upstairs for her. She looks like a little girl playing house," laughed Silas. "I think she is going to love being in the apartment. The only problem will be getting her out long enough to do her job."

"Don't worry about it," said May. "She'll settle in soon. I know how she feels. It's great to have your own space."

"I guess," agreed Silas. "Jamie and I were so close, we never minded having each other around, but when we moved out, we each found our own place. I think Jamie was looking to start a family. He wanted to be prepared."

"Jamie and April will be over in a while. They are going to be here to show Dad and Mother the way to Jamie's house," said May. "I didn't want to give Mother the chance to tell me what a mistake I am making."

Silas pulled her into his arms and kissed her. "It's just for a few days," he said. "They will be gone and we will have the rest of our lives to be together."

"Yes, we will," agreed May, kissing him again.

～

April and Jamie arrived at Silas and May's place at a few minutes before six. They all settled in the living room to wait. May brought in glasses of iced tea, and they settled back to talk until their company arrived.

"Are you all set for the wedding?" May asked April.

"Yes, I have a new dress. I would have liked to make a marriage bracelet, but I didn't have time," said April.

"You can make one after the wedding and have Derrick Bear bless it for you," said May.

"I suppose," said April. "It just doesn't seem the same somehow. Did you finish yours?"

"Yes," said May. "It was close. After getting knocked on the head and going to the hospital, I was afraid I wouldn't finish it in time."

"I hear a car," said Silas. He and Jamie went to the door to see who was there.

Silas looked out the door. "It's your folks," said Silas.

May and April joined them, and they all went out on the porch.

Serin was out first and opened the door and released the boys from their seats. Autumn started toward the porch.

"Aunt May! Aunt May!" called the boys as they dashed around their mother and toward the porch; they threw themselves at May. Both of them were hugging her tightly.

May laughed and hugged them just as tightly. She pulled them over to the swing and sat down with one on each side of her. Silas smiled at the sight. May was so happy surrounded by children's love.

"Don't smother your aunt, boys," said Autumn.

"They are fine," said May, hugging the boys when they started to pull away at their mother's words.

They settled back at her side happily. Serin frowned and gave Autumn a stern look, which she ignored. April had gone over to greet their parents. Guy gave April a hug and started for the porch and May. April turned to her mother and leaning in kissed her cheek.

Violet frowned at April. "Why do you have to be in such a hurry to marry?" she asked. "Shouldn't you finish your classes first?"

"I love Jamie, Mother. I have finished my classes. I have to do an internship next."

"How will you do an internship here?" asked Violet.

"I already have an internship arranged. I will be interning for Glen Black Feather. He is the best lawyer in the state," said April.

Violet frowned but didn't say anything else. She looked over at May who was still busy with the boys. It really made her angry when the boys made such a fuss over May when they barely tolerated her. She didn't seem to be aware that she was to blame for their attitude toward her. She never showed them the unconditional love they received from May.

Guy had reached the porch. He greeted May and leaned in and kissed her cheek.

"Hi, Dad," said May with a smile. She stayed where she was and held onto the boys.

Violet came upon the porch and looked down her nose at May. "I see you have what you have always wanted," said Violet. "You swore when we moved away from here, you would be back here someday."

"Yes," agreed May. "I have just what I want. I have a man who loves me, and I love him. I knew I was leaving him behind when we moved. I always wanted to be back here with him."

Silas squeezed her shoulder. He was standing behind the

swing and directly behind her and the boys. Violet gave him a hard look, but she didn't say anything. Guy came over and took her arm and steered her away from May. May looked back over her shoulder and smiled at Silas.

April came onto the porch and faced their parents. "Dad, you and Mother will be staying with Jamie and me. Autumn and Serin and the boys will stay here with May and Silas."

"Why can't we all stay together?" asked Violet.

"Because neither of us has enough room for all of you at once, and Gunner only has one bedroom," said April.

Gunner and Brenda drove up into the yard and came over to greet everyone.

The boys jumped up and hugged Gunner and then snuggled up next to May again. Silas smiled when the boys sat close to May again. They knew she would look out for them and protect them from their grandmother.

Guy shook hands with Gunner, Jamie, and Silas. He gave Brenda a hug and told her he was glad she and Gunner had gotten together. May noticed he did not say anything to Silas or Jamie. She pushed the thought away. She was glad Gunner was going to walk her down the aisle.

Silas could hear May's thoughts, and he didn't want her to be sad. "It doesn't matter, my woodland sprite. We do not need his approval. I think he is trying to keep your mother from being upset. He doesn't want to draw her attention to us and cause her to flare up. We have each other and they will soon be gone," thought Silas.

"I love you. I can't wait until we are joined in all ways. You make me complete," thought May with a smile.

Silas smiled at her and squeezed her shoulder again.

"Well, If you are ready, April and I will show you the way to our house," said Jamie. He looked at Guy and Violet inquiringly.

Guy nodded and taking Violet's arm, told everyone good-night and that he would see them the next day. He led the way to his car and helped Violet in before she could say anything else. Jamie and April told everyone goodnight and went to Jamie's truck to lead the way.

May relaxed some after her parents left. She told Serin and Autumn about the birthday party at Doris's the next day.

"We don't have a gift," objected Autumn.

"We have until eleven in the morning," said Gunner. "How old is Orin?"

"I think he is six or seven. I'm not sure," said May.

"Brenda and I will pick up a couple of gifts in the morning," said Gunner.

"Alright," said the boys. "We get to go on pony rides."

"Will it be safe?" asked Autumn.

"They will be well looked after," said May. "Silas and I will be there, and you and Serin can come, too. If you want to come."

"I will come along," said Serin.

"I think I will stay here and rest," said Autumn.

May didn't say anything, but she couldn't understand how Autumn could hold herself distant from two such wonderful boys. She gave the boys an extra squeeze. They both smiled up at her happily.

"Are you hungry?" asked May. Both boys nodded their heads. "Let's go see what we can find to eat," said May, rising and taking the boys' hands and leading the way inside.

"Serin, there are two bedrooms and a bathroom down the hall. You and Autumn can have one and put the boys in the other," said May.

Silas and Gunner went with Serin to bring in their bags. Autumn and Brenda followed May and the boys into the kitchen and dining area.

May smiled at Shala. Shala had seen everyone arriving and had come in the back door to prepare a meal for them. "Thanks, Shala," said May. "Boys, this is Shala. She has prepared you a delicious meal. Shala, this is my friend Brenda and my sister Autumn and her boys, Stan and Gus."

"I'm glad to meet you all. I fixed my brother's favorite meal. I hope the boys will enjoy it. There is chocolate cake for dessert," she said with a smile.

"Alright!" said the boys together. May, Brenda, and Shala laughed, even Autumn managed a small smile.

The guys joined them and, after taking the boys to wash their hands, everyone sat down to a meal of chicken nuggets, mashed potatoes, and green beans. The boys happily dug in, and the adults seemed to be enjoying their meal also.

"Join us, Shala," said May.

"I already ate at my apartment," said Shala with pride.

May grinned at Silas, and he smiled back at her. They both knew how much pride Shala had in her simple statement.

After the boys enjoyed their cake and helped clear the table, May took them to show them where they would be sleeping. Shala had unpacked their bags and turned down their bed while they had been eating.

"You can watch television for a little. Then you are going to have to have to get some sleep so you will be rested for your pony rides tomorrow," said May.

She took the boys into the living room where everyone was sitting talking. The boys sat down beside Gunner and started watching the television. The others had turned it on and were not paying any attention to it. May saw there was a comedy on, so she didn't say anything about the boys watching it.

Shala came in and addressed May. "I have the dishes in

the dishwasher. Do you need me to do anything else?" she asked.

"No," said May. "Thank you for coming over. Enjoy your night," Shala smiled and left.

Autumn was watching them with a frown. May glanced at her but did not comment.

"You were lucky to find Shala," said Brenda.

"Yes, I was," agreed May. "She is Rosa's granddaughter. She recommended her."

"Who is Rosa?" asked Brenda.

"She is Silas and Jamie's second mother," said May with a smile at Silas. Silas smiled at May. He remembered introducing Rosa to May in just that way.

"Are you all set for day after tomorrow?" asked Gunner.

"Yes, I can't wait," said May with a loving look at Silas. The look was returned in full.

"Do you still want me to walk you down the aisle?" asked Gunner.

"Yes," May nodded emphatically. "Dad is going to walk April down, but I want you to walk me down."

"Okay, I was just checking," said Gunner. "I am honored to be your escort."

"Thank you," said May.

Serin rose. "Come on, boys, it's time for bed." The boys rose and followed him without protest. He looked surprised. May smiled. Her talk with the boys earlier had done its job. She lay back against Silas and enjoyed feeling his arms tighten around her.

Serin was back shortly. "The boys went straight to bed," he said. He still looked surprised. May didn't say anything,

"Serin told me you were setting up trust funds for Gus and Stan," said Autumn.

"Yes, I am," agreed May. "My lawyer is handling them.

They should be done in a few days. Glen Black Feather will be in charge and will be one of the trustees. Serin will be the other trustee. The funds will be added to every year, and the boys will be able to use them for college, and they will be turned over to them in full when they turn twenty-five."

"Why are you doing it?" asked Autumn.

May looked at her in surprise. "Because they are my nephews, and I love them. I want them to get the best start in life possible."

"Doesn't Silas object to you giving away all of that money?" asked Autumn.

"I support May's decision completely," said Silas.

Autumn still looked like she couldn't understand why anyone would give away all of that money, but she didn't say anything else about it. "I am tired. I think I will go to bed," said Autumn rising.

"I'll go with you," said Serin. "It's been a long day. Thank you, May and Silas for, having us."

"You are family. You are always welcome," said Silas.

"Have a good night," said May as Serin came over and kissed her cheek before leaving to follow Autumn into the bedroom.

"Autumn sure lucked out when she ended up with him," said Gunner after Serin and Autumn were gone. May just nodded but didn't say anything.

"We need to be going, too. We have to go find a couple of presents in the morning," said Brenda. "If you need any help, call me."

"Thank you, I will," promised May as she and Silas went to walk Brenda and Gunner out. They came back in, and May gave a tired sigh and turned into Silas' arms.

Silas kissed her and held her close. "It will soon be over," he said.

"I know," said May. "I am going to miss the boys when they are gone, but the rest of the drama I can do without."

Silas took her hand and led her to the bedroom. "I can help you relax," said Silas.

"I know you can," agreed May. "I am counting on your relaxing treatment."

She melted into his arms, and they were soon in bed and wrapped up in each other. May was feeling no stress. Silas' treatment worked fine.

CHAPTER 15

*G*unner and Brenda came early the next morning. They had brought gifts for Orin. May and Silas had eaten early with the boys. Serin and Autumn had just come into the kitchen and were getting some coffee.

Brenda opened the bags and showed them the wrapping paper, bows, and tape. "Do you have any scissors, May?" asked Brenda.

"Sure," answered May. She looked in a drawer and retrieved some scissors. She handed them to Brenda.

Gus and Stan were crowed around Brenda trying to see what the gifts were. Brenda smiled at them and opened the other bag.

"Wow," said the boys as they looked at the gifts. One was a police car. It had flashing lights and a siren. The doors would open and close, also. The boys loved it.

Gunner laughed. "I guess I know what to get them on their next birthday,"

The other gift was a bucket of building blocks. The boys liked it, too but not as much as the police car. They lay everything on the table and started cutting paper and wrapping the gifts. They put tags on both gifts. They wrote, "to Orin from Gus and Stan." They had both gifts from both boys. They didn't want any arguments about who was giving what.

The boys were dressed in some old jeans and a button-up, long-sleeved shirts. The shirt was May's suggestion. She did not want the boys to get blistered. They were wearing tennis shoes. Gunner came forward with another bag. He opened it and presented each boy with a cowboy hat. "These will protect your faces," said Gunner. The boys hugged Gunner and let him show them how to wear the hats. They strutted around, proudly showing off their hats. Even Autumn had to smile at their pleased expressions.

"Are you two going?" May asked Gunner. "I'm sure you will be welcome. It will be a good chance to meet a lot of neighbors before the wedding."

Gunner looked at Brenda. She nodded. "Sure," he said. "I would like to meet everyone."

"Autumn, why don't you come with us? You will enjoy watching the boys ride the ponies," said May.

Autumn paused for a minute, looking around. "Okay," she said with a shrug.

So, they ended up with a three-car parade on their way to Mark and Doris's house. Silas and May led the way.

There were a lot of cars parked to one side when they arrived. They pulled in and parked in line with the other cars. Gunner and Serin followed them. They all piled out and looked around in amazement. There looked like people everywhere. They started toward the house. They could see where a place had been set up for the pony rides.

"I'm going to see if I can help Logan and Marcel with the pony rides," said Silas. "Gunner, you want to come with me?"

"Sure," said Gunner. "Serin, why don't you and the boys come with us? You may get your pony rides early."

Silas gave May a quick kiss and led the way to where his cousins were giving out pony rides. Gunner, Serin and the boys followed him.

May and Brenda along with Autumn went on to the house. "This is some place," said Autumn looking around in awe.

"Yes, it is beautiful," agreed May and Brenda.

They were greeted on the porch by Doris, Daisy, and Willow. As they greeted everyone and May introduced them, Dawn, Daisy's daughter, came from inside. She had her daughter's hands in hers, leading them outside. "Now, go get your pony rides," she said. "I'm tired of listening to you whine."

The girls gave their mother a look then took off running toward the pony rides. Dawn turned to the others on the porch.

"I thought you told them they couldn't ride the ponies," said Daisy with an amused look on her face.

"I know, but I was punishing myself more than them," said Dawn.

Daisy laughed. "You have just learned a fundamental fact of raising children. Never give them a punishment you can't endure."

"We'll have to remember that," said Doris. The other ladies nodded their agreement.

May and Brenda gave Doris the gifts to be added to the pile already waiting for Orin's attention.

"We have the community center all decorated for tomorrow," said Daisy. "Did you get your bracelet finished?"

"Yes, Silas finished his, too," said May.

"You didn't show it to him, did you?" asked Willow.

"No, we haven't shown either of them," assured May. "Where's Camille?" asked May.

"She's sleeping. She will be awake soon," said Willow.

"Would you ladies like to come inside and get some ice tea?" asked Doris.

"Sure," said May. They all followed Doris inside. May had been there before, so she was prepared for the inside. Autumn and Brenda looked around in awe.

"This is the most beautiful house I have ever seen," said Autumn. Brenda nodded agreement.

"Thank you," said Doris with a smile. "I am still getting used to it myself. Mark had it built for us."

They all went into the dining room, and Doris started pouring glasses of tea. May went over and helped her hand them out. They all took seats at the table. They were starting to drink their tea when they heard someone call hello. Doris stood up and looked to see who it was.

"We are in here," called Doris.

April came into the room. "Jamie went down to the pony rides and told me to come on in," said April.

May stood up. "Doris, this is my sister April. She is marrying Jamie tomorrow. April, this is Doris Black Feather. Beside her are Daisy Black Feather and Willow Black Feather."

"Wow," said April. "I am glad to meet Uncle Glen's family. I'm going to be interning for him. I'm really looking forward to working for him. I have had a lot of respect for him ever since I attended his lectures at the university."

Daisy laughed. "I'm sure he appreciates your enthusiasm."

Glen came into the dining room. He headed straight to Daisy and kissed her. Daisy smiled. I thought you were helping with the pony rides," she said.

"They don't need me," said Glen. "They seem to have almost as many adults as children. They can handle it."

He looked around and nodded to the ladies. He spotted April. "I see you have met my new intern. Hello, April. Would you like a glass of tea?" he asked.

Doris jumped up. "I'm sorry, I haven't offered you anything. Would you like some tea?"

"Yes, please," said April.

"What about you, Dad?" asked Doris.

"Yes, I believe I could use some refreshment after all of those pony rides," said Glen. Doris brought two glasses of tea and handed them to April and Glen.

"Are you going to serve the cake and ice cream in here," asked April.

"No. Mark and Logan set up a tent and tables and chairs outside. Mark said he was not going to have sticky fingerprints all over the place until they belonged to our own little sticky fingers," laughed Doris.

"I don't blame him," said Dawn. "Children have no idea how to not touch,"

"You learn to live with it," said Daisy. "They are worth a few sticky fingerprints."

Glen put an arm around her shoulder. "Yes, they are," he agreed.

Mark and Logan came into the dining room. Mark went straight to Doris and kissed her, and Logan went to Willow and kissed her both wives smiled up at their husbands.

"Is everyone having fun?" asked Doris.

"They are loving the pony rides. The ones waiting their turns have been playing tag," said Logan.

"Gus and Stan fit right in," said Mark. "I think Sarah has a bit of a crush on Gus," said Mark.

"What, she is only five years old," said Doris.

"She sure was watching him," said Logan.

"It's probably because he is new. She is just curious," said Doris. Logan shrugged his shoulders and let it go.

Mark gave her shoulders a squeeze. "Relax, he's just teasing you," said Mark.

Doris gave Logan a look. "That's my baby sister your talking about," she said.

"I'm sorry," said Logan. "I didn't mean to upset you."

"I'm sorry. I shouldn't be so touchy," said Doris.

"Do you need us to take the pizzas out and get set up for cake and ice cream?" asked Mark.

"Yeah, we can have pizza first and then cake and ice cream. After they finish eating, he can open his presents. We can take his presents out and set them up on the table under the tent," said Doris.

"We can help," said May.

She and the other ladies all started forward to help, all except Willow. Camille cried, and Willow went to see about her. The others followed Doris and helped her carry the presents out to the tent.

Glen went with Mark and Logan to carry out the pizza, cake, and drinks. Mark put the candles on the cake and laid the lighter beside it. Then he picked the lighter up and put it in his pocket.

"Good idea," said Glen. "You don't need to leave temptation laying around."

Doris and the ladies brought a box of party favors out and put them on the table with the gifts.

Logan went and told the ones at the pony rides to stop for a while for pizza and cake. They helped the last riders off the ponies and all headed for the tent. They gathered up children as they went. Glen and Mark had put pizza on each plate. They were all ready to sing "Happy Birthday" as soon as the children finished the pizza. While they were eating the pizza, the cake was brought in and the candles lit. Daisy led the singing and they all joined in. Orin blew out the candles. He grinned big when he blew them all out.

Mark started cutting cake, and all of the ladies started passing it around. Logan and Jamie passed out ice cream. The kids dug in. As soon as he was finished with his cake and ice cream, Doris and Daisy led Orin to the table of gifts. The other children gathered around to see what he was getting. Orin was amazed at so many presents. He had never been so fussed over. It took some getting used to.

He loved everything he received, but as soon as he was done opening presents, he ran to play with his friends and to have more pony rides,

The ladies gathered up presents and took them inside. A couple of them brought trash cans and collected paper and paper plates and ice cream cups. They filled two trash cans with trash. Silas and Serin came and helped Mark and Logan take in chairs and put them in the garage. They folded up tables and put them in the garage also. Next, they took down the tent and stored it.

In no time at all, with all of them helping, they had everything cleared away and were ready to sit and rest and visit.

They all sat on the porch and watched the children run and play. Logan and Dawn's husband, Hank, were continuing the pony rides. They had brought some different ponies out so the first ones could rest.

After another hour, May stirred and looked around. "We need to round up the boys and head home. We have a lot to do before the wedding tomorrow," she said.

Silas and Serin went to find the boys and brought them back to the porch. Sarah and Orin followed them to the porch. Doris noticed Sarah was watching Gus closely. Orin came and thanked them for the gifts. He invited them to come and play anytime.

May and Silas started for their car after telling everyone goodbye. They all assured them they would see each other at the wedding. Sarah sat on the porch and watched Gus and Stan get into their parents' car to leave. Doris came over and sat beside her.

"Are you alright, Sarah?" asked Doris.

Sarah nodded. Her eyes followed the car Gus was in until it was out of sight. Sarah sighed and looked at Doris.

"He and I will be together someday," she said.

She left a stunned Doris and went inside.

Doris looked at Glen sitting by Daisy.

"Dad," she said. Glen looked at her inquiringly. "Is there any chance the Larks family is related to Moon Walking?" she asked.

Glen looked surprised. "It is possible," he replied. "Why?"

"Sarah just said something that reminded me of Moon Walking," said Doris.

~

When May and Silas went home, Gunner and Serin followed them. April and Jamie went to their place. April felt guilty for leaving her parents alone for so long. May called April and told her she could bring them over to visit for a while.

"No," said April. "I am going to get some rest. We can come over in the morning, and maybe Mother and Autumn will help us arrange our hair tor the wedding."

"Okay, we will see you in the morning," said May.

She turned to the others and smiled.

"April said she is going to get some rest and will see us in the morning," said May.

May looked at Stan and Gus. "Would you guys like to be in my wedding?" she asked.

"What would we have to do?" asked Stan.

"You would walk down the aisle together carrying our marriage bracelets on small pillows. When you get to the front and we take the bracelets, you can go and sit with your dad. He will save you a seat."

Gus and Stan looked at each other and nodded. "We can do it," they agreed.

May came over and gave each of them a hug. "Thank you," she said.

"We are going, so you can get some rest," said Gunner, taking Brenda's hand and helping her to her feet. "We will see you in the morning."

Silas came over and shook Gunner's hand and hugged Brenda. May hugged both Brenda and Gunner.

When Gunner and Brenda left, Serin and Autumn headed to their rooms after saying goodnight and taking the boys to their room and seeing them to bed.

When May and Silas started to their room, Gus came back out and asked for a glass of water. May took him to the kitchen for water, and Silas went on to the bedroom. When May handed Gus the water, he took a sip and looked at May.

"Is something wrong?" asked May.

Gus looked up at her solemnly. "How do you know if you are in love?" he asked.

"You have a feeling in your heart," said May.

Gus thought about it for a minute, then nodded. "Sarah and I are going to be together someday," he said. He handed the glass of water to May and went to bed.

May emptied the glass and put it in the sink. She went into the bedroom and went to Silas and hugged him.

"Is something wrong?" asked Silas.

"Gus just informed me he and Sarah are going to be together someday," said May.

Silas held her close. "Who knows," he said. "Anything is possible with the Great Spirit. We don't have to think about it now. We have a wedding to attend. We should focus on it for now. We have years before we have to think about Sarah and Gus."

"You are right," agreed May. "Let's focus on now,"

They took their own advice and focused on themselves and now.

The next morning found everyone getting ready for the wedding. After Gunner arrived, Silas took his clothes and went to Jamie's house to get ready. April had brought her clothes and came with her mother to May's house. Autumn and Violet helped all the ladies fix their hair and then fixed each other's hair. Serin helped Gus and Stan get ready, and Shala provided breakfast and coffee for anyone who asked for it. May and April were too nervous to eat. They were afraid to drink coffee. They thought it would make them more nervous. They were finally ready. Everyone was dressed and ready. Serin and Autumn took the boys and Gunner and Brenda took May. April drove with her Mother. Gunner led the way so May could show them where to go.

When they arrived, Jamie and Silas were already there. May spotted their car and truck. Derrick Bear Met them as they went in. He had already had Jamie fill out the marriage license, but April had to sign it. He took the signed license and went into the other room to prepare for the ceremony.

Autumn and Violet were escorted to their seats. May peeped in the door; she saw Silas and Jamie up front by

Derrick. The place was packed. She drew back before she was seen.

"I love you," thought May.

"I love you, my woodland sprite," said Silas.

May felt much calmer after speaking with Silas.

The music started and Brenda was the first to go down the aisle. April was next being escorted by her Dad. Serin was staying with the boys to tell them when to go. They had seats saved for them up front. Gunner and May were next to walk forward. When they reached the front Gunner passed her hand to Silas and kissed her on her cheek. He then went to sit beside his Mother and Dad.

Derrick went through the ceremony quickly. He had them all say their vows and exchange rings. Then it was time for the bracelets. Gus and Stan walked down to the front side by side. Serin took a seat to wait for them to finish. May smiled at them, and they smiled back.

Silas took his bracelet first and turned to May. May saw it for the first time. It had two hearts joined by a cord. One heart had an "M" in it. The other heart had an "S."

Silas tied the bracelet on May's arm. He looked into May's eyes and said, "The memory of our love has joined our hearts for eternity."

May's bracelet was on a tan strap. There was an "I" at the top, a heart in the middle, and "U" at the bottom.

May took her bracelet and tied it on Silas' arm. She looked into Silas' eyes and said, "You are always in my heart. Love's memory brought us through the years. The love in our hearts will take us on the most amazing journey of our lives. I love you."

Silas leaned forward and kissed her soundly. He then drew back and said, "I love you."

Derrick Bear raised his hand for attention."We ask the

Great Spirit to bless these bracelets and the couple wearing them. May the love they weaved into them grow stronger as the years pass. I now pronounce you man and wife, Jamie and April, and Silas and May. You may now kiss your brides."

"He already did," said a young voice. Everyone laughed, but Jamie and Silas did not hear they were doing as Derrick said and kissing their wives.

THE END

Dear reader,

We hope you enjoyed reading *Love's Memory*. Please take a moment to leave a review in Amazon, even if it's a short one. Your opinion is important to us.

Discover more books by Betty McLain at https://www.nextchapter.pub/authors/betty-mclain

Want to know when one of our books is free or discounted for Kindle? Join the newsletter at http://eepurl.com/bqqB3H

Best regards,

Betty McLain and the Next Chapter Team

ABOUT THE AUTHOR

With five children, ten grandchildren and six great-grandchil-dren, I have a very busy life, but reading and writing have always been a very large and enjoyable part of my life. I have been writing since I was very young. I kept notebooks with my stories in them private. I didn't share them with anyone. They were all handwritten because I was unable to type. We lived in the country, and I had to do most of my writing at night. My days were busy helping with my brothers and sister. I also helped Mom with the garden and canning food for our family. Even though I was tired, I still managed to get my thoughts down on paper at night.

When I married and began raising my family, I continued writing my stories while helping my children through school and into their own lives and families. My sister was the only one to read my stories. She was very encouraging. When my youngest daughter started college, I decided to go to college myself. I had taken my GED at an earlier date and only had to take a class to pass my college entrance tests. I passed with flying colors and even managed to get a partial scholarship. I took computer classes to learn typing. The English and litera-ture classes helped me to polish my stories.

I found public speaking was not for me. I was much more comfortable with the written word, but researching and writing the speeches was helpful. I could use information to build a story. I still managed to put my own spin on the essays.

I finished college with an associate degree and a 3.4 GPA. I had several awards, including President's List, Dean's List, and Faculty List. The school experience helped me gain more confidence in my writing. I want to thank my English teacher in college for giving me more confidence in my writing by telling me that I had a good imagination. She said I told an interesting story. My daughter, who is a very good writer and has books of her own published, convinced me to have some of my stories published. She used her experience self-publishing to publish my stories for me. The first time I held one of my books in my hands and looked at my name on it as author, I was so proud. They were very well received. This was encouragement enough to convince me to continue writing and publishing. I have been building my library of books written by Betty McLain since then. I also wrote and illustrated several children's books.

Being able to type my stories opened up a whole new world for me. Having access to a computer helped me to look up anything I needed to know and expanded my ability to keep writing my books. Joining Facebook and making friends all over the world expanded my outlook considerably. I was able to understand many different lifestyles and incorporate them in my ideas.

I have heard the saying, "Watch out what you say, and don't make the writer mad, you may end up in a book being eliminated." It is true. All of life is there to stimulate your imagination. It is fun to sit and think about how a thought can be changed to develop a story and to watch the story develop and come alive in your mind. When I get started, the stories almost write themselves; I just have to get all of it down as I think it before it is gone.

I love knowing the stories I have written are being read

and enjoyed by others. It is awe-inspiring to look at the books and think, "I wrote that."

I look forward to many more years of putting my stories out there and hope the people reading my books are looking forward to reading them as much.

Lightning Source UK Ltd.
Milton Keynes UK
UKHW021006060121
376497UK00008B/426/J